ANCIENT ADVENTURES

KENT

Edited By Donna Samworth

Years of  Young**Writers**

First published in Great Britain in 2016 by:

Young**Writers**

x

Coltsfoot Drive
Peterborough
PE2 9BF
Telephone: 01733 890066
Website: www.youngwriters.co.uk

SB ISBN 978-1-78624-343-0
Printed and bound in the UK by BookPrintingUK
Website: www.bookprintinguk.com
YB0276H

FOREWORD

Welcome, Reader!
Have you ever wondered what it would be like if you stepped back in time? Well, for Young Writers' latest competition, we asked our writers nationwide to travel back in time and create a story of up to 100 words with a beginning, middle and end – a hard task indeed!

I am delighted to present to you 'Ancient Adventures – Kent', a collection of ingenious storytelling that covers a whole host of different topics. Just like me, you will be transported to all types of different adventures and, I'm sure, will learn something new with each story you read. Perhaps you'll enjoy taking a trip to the future, be amazed by a mythical legend or find yourself getting all wrapped up with the mummies in ancient Egypt!

You may also find that this anthology will take you on a roller-coaster ride of emotions that pull on your heart strings, make you laugh out loud, or maybe terrify you to your very core, so be warned!

The standard of entries, as always, was extremely high so I'd like to congratulate all the talented writers featured in this collection and, as you step back in time, I hope you find as much enjoyment reading these mini sagas as I did.

Donna Samworth

CONTENTS

Burnt Oak Primary School, Gillingham

Isaac Olajide (10)	26
Courtney Irwin (8)	26
Joshua Tyrone (10)	27
Tyler Woollett (10)	27
Kenzly Wells (9)	28
Hallee Wells (9)	28
Shania Stone (8)	29
Bobby Brinn (9)	29
Faith Julie Ann Dykes (11)	30
Paris Purdue (10)	30
Joeb Church (8)	31
Alfie Delaney Dugard (10)	31
Sophia Watkins (8)	32
Maddison Turner (9)	32
Emmanuella Ikwetie (9)	33
Adelina Bajrami (9)	33
Nicole Worship (9)	34
Johnny Harbard (9)	34
Zaina Khan (9)	35
Ellie Prebble (10)	35
Max Piper (8)	36
Keelan Philpott (10)	36
Eve Hooper (9)	37
Shana Poole	37
Kristen Woolley (9)	38
Katlyn Savage (10)	38
Janice Ighauodha (8)	39
Jasmine White (10)	39
Saphanya Philpott (9)	40
Raiah Russell-Heard (10)	40
Alfie Hatcher (9)	41
Tracy Lartey (9)	41
Yajna Rungien	42
Ryan Jay Hart (10)	42
Jake Moseley (8)	43
Danielle Cole (10)	43
Calum Groot (9)	44
Jayden Taylor-Harding (9)	44
Keana Roxanne Melo (9)	45
Taylor Bullas (7)	45
Molly Bailey (9)	46
Inês Henriques (8)	46
Jason Thuku (9)	47
Arthur Patey (7)	47
Louis Stuart Mills (9)	48
Lauren Groot (8)	48
Adam Hewing-Everitt (8)	49
Ethan Gosney (8)	49
Ella Chelsea Szalajko (8)	50
Isabelle Rose Ongley (8)	50
Ellie Beth Hales-Ward (8)	51
Charlotte Elizabeth Tucker (7)	51
Bnyad Hawkar Salar (9)	52
Cassie Owen (8)	52
Jessica Rhianne Poole (9)	53
Domas Urbonas	53
Millie Herve (8)	54
Hannah Rebecca-May Joseph (9)	54
Ruby Skillings (8)	55
David Gracio (10)	55
Lauren Springham (9)	56
Grace Oliver (7)	56
Louie Allen-Fox (9)	57
Izzie Baker (8)	57
Jakub Henry Darmovzal-Chadwick (8)	58
Frankie Jane Pearl Douglas (8)	58
Saffron Tyrone (8)	59
Samira Mariam Jah (8)	59
Sophie Woollett (9)	60
Lillie-Rose Manley (11)	60
Dillan Hedges (8)	61
Shannan Lee Bridget Batson (10)	61
Ellie Jefford (9)	62
Michaela Mardel (8)	62
Patryk Bielski (9)	63
Jasmine Thuku (11)	63

Yaashwant Selvaradjou (9)	64	Rayan Aziz (9)	83
Kieran Waters (10)	64	Nuyem Chemjong (9)	83
Lillie Spinks (7)	65	Anevay Gravesande-Whyte (8)	84
Melissa Woolley (10)	66		
Courtney Hook (11)	66		
Kelly Xu (8)	67		
Abigail Westcott (10)	67		

The Gordon Schools Federation, Rochester

Jack Norfolk (10)	85
Ella Wills (10)	85
Ellie Louise Fox (9)	86
Rubie Harrs (10)	86

East Stour Primary School, Ashford

Paul Manu (9)	68	Chelsy Victoria Smith (9)	87
Frankie Jada Griffiths (9)	68	Jake Mark Lee Thiselton (9)	87
Jack George (8)	69	George Denniss-Baker (9)	88
Samantha Knapman (8)	69	Grace Jagger (8)	88
Joseph Barrett (9)	70	Daisy-Mae Scott (9)	89
Lois-Grace Knight (9)	70	Felix Condy (9)	89
Louise April Gadd (8)	71	Tia Li Riley (9)	90
Holly Apps (8)	71	Victoria Ward (8)	90
Jake Freeman (9)	72	Amelia Pollard (9)	91
Tommy Randall (8)	72	Shakira Bah (8)	91
Orlando Caka (9)	73	Joseph Sobanjo (9)	92
Macy Patterson (9)	73	Lee Jones (9)	92
Darcey Taylor-Kirk (9)	74	Ben Penfold (8)	93
Keira Harman (8)	74	Lucca Wade (9)	93
Ellie Shaw (9)	75	Tia Venn (9)	94
Chloe Louise Hughes (8)	75	Kian Terry (10)	94
Isobel Boorman (9)	76	Evie Lipscombe (9)	95
Millie Smith (9)	76	Layla Lola Jones (10)	95
Shaun Ellesmere (8)	77	Ryan Pearton (9)	96
Alex Ojo (8)	77	Lauren Stevens (10)	96
Freddie Masters (8)	78	Roshan Ahmed Shebani (9)	97
Rebecca Chapple (8)	78	Ben Titterington (9)	97
Jessica Griffiths (9)	79	Nestor Furst (9)	98
Kyle Endicott (9)	79	Ria Sampla (10)	98
Ella Darlington (9)	80	Jude Johnson (9)	99
Nandika Thileepan (9)	80	Billy Hicks (9)	99
Casey Marlow (9)	81	Chloe Randall (8)	100
Beatrice McCarthy (9)	81	Hayden Foakes (9)	100
Kelsie-Jae Hodges (9)	82	Aaron Uzomah Aguele (9)	101
Samina Thebe (9)	82	Isobelle Higgins (10)	101

Rhys Spencer (9)	102
Sanjana Arumulla (10)	102
Olivia Nangle (10)	103
Charlie Langridge (9)	104
Emma Rose Hill (9)	104
Dara Stoyanova (10)	105
Zhi Hong Weng (10)	105
Ellie-Mai Woods (10)	106
Andrew Ferguson (9)	106
Carys Ann (10)	107
Joshua Achunine (9)	107
Vincent Kwiatkowski (10)	108
Trinity Elizabeth Grant (9)	108
Jack Younger-Munn (10)	109
Olivia Shanahan (10)	109
Magdalena Jedrzejczyk (10)	110
Daisy Rose Bibby (9)	110
Ellis Dunbar (10)	111
Katalina Espineira (8)	111
Tia Louise Conway (8)	112
Evie Mitchell (10)	112
Esme Margaret Phillipson (10)	113
Harrison Dallas (9)	113
Sally Wells (10)	114
Caydee-Lee Roberts (9)	114
Jorja Tuite (10)	115
Jordan Kweku Mensah (8)	115
Sophie Crosbie (9)	116
Favio Sequeira (8)	116
James Reach (9)	117
Harry Dunk (9)	117
Mia Sanghera (9)	118
Emily Hawes (10)	118
Grace-Olivia Putt (8)	119
Megan Pinnick (9)	120
Adam Deans (9)	120
Katie Smith (9)	121

THE
MINI SAGAS

The Bear

'It's so foggy out here,' said Brian.

'We're only here to hunt a bear,' answered Jay. 'See, I can see bear tracks.'

After about twenty minutes they finally found the bear's cave so they went in, lit a match and right before their eyes was a kodiak bear. His eyes were yellow and he had black fur. Suddenly, he charged. Jay slashed him with his axe but it didn't do anything. The bear called more bears and more and more. They tried with their axes but absolutely nothing happened. They knew they were surrounded.

'Help now, please!' said Brian...

Loye Iyanda (9)
Benedict House Preparatory School, Sidcup

Betrayal By The King

It was a normal day in Great Glen and a boy called Jack walked along, but there was something weird going on. Henry VIII was strolling into people's houses, taking food, and strolling on. The villagers were very upset because they didn't have much food and people were muttering, 'Why is he taking it?'

King Henry was planning a feast with the other monarchs tonight. Jack suggested they disguise themselves and attend the banquet. They had a lovely time and ate all the food. The government decided Jack should be king and have a new royal family.

Rowan Jonathan Daniel Threader (7)
Benedict House Preparatory School, Sidcup

The Cleo!

Cleopatra bossed everyone around and she was the last pharaoh. She bossed everyone around so she could relax whilst everyone else worked. She just slept and slept. One day, she woke up and she was in a tomb. Cleo couldn't get out for two years. Finally she got out then Cleo went to Ancient Egypt. Everyone was shocked. Someone shouted, 'She's alive!' Everyone hugged Cleo and Cleo started bossing everyone around. Soon everyone wanted a new pharaoh. Cleo started crying whilst everyone was crowding her.
The following week she passed away and the people cried for years.

Kannisha Shanmugarajah (7)
Benedict House Preparatory School, Sidcup

The Mummy Returns

One day a person called Nick was going to the toilet. He came outside and turned into a mummy but he fell into a hole. The mummy buried himself up. *Stomp! Stomp! Stomp!* Footsteps were coming closer. Suddenly, a pirate got the mummy out and he travelled with him to Egypt. When they got to Egypt, the Egyptian man found them and sent them to the Pharaoh. The Pharaoh was not there so the visitor took his place. When the bad man went to get gold, the mummy stopped him.

Sophie Li (7)
Benedict House Preparatory School, Sidcup

Daisy's Riding Lesson

Daisy was at the stables with her best friend Stacey. She was delighted when they started riding their ponies! But when a cat and mouse ran across the riding arena, Pepper, Daisy's pony, got scared and jumped sideways. Daisy fell off with a shriek. She was not moving!

'Daisy, are you all right?' Stacey cried.

'I am scared,' Daisy whispered.

'Too scared to ride?' asked Stacey anxiously.

'No, no,' replied Daisy. 'Not of riding, but I am afraid of mice.' Then she got up, caught Pepper and rode happily on. The cat and mouse were gone.

Tanya Mannio (8)
Benedict House Preparatory School, Sidcup

Tutankhamun And The Invisible Man

One day, Tutankhamun was walking dreamily through one of his beautiful gardens. Suddenly, he heard a voice whispering behind him, 'If you don't give me your golden crown, you will die on your 19th birthday.'

Tutankhamun was terrified and turned around but he could not see anybody. He stammered, 'Who's there?' The leaves ruffled around him and he felt a current of icy air touching his face.

The whisper returned, 'I'm the spirit of the North. I want the crown so that I can be pharaoh!'

Tut exclaimed, 'My father gave me this crown and you can never have it!'

Clara Thea Vernis (8)
Benedict House Preparatory School, Sidcup

Grimbeard The Vicious And Vile

As Grimbeard set off to raid, the Hooligan tribe shouted, 'Bring us food, bring us loot, go, go, go, you can't choose!'
After a day on the sea, Grimbeard, the vicious but clever, realised something; he realised the driver of the ship took them the wrong way. After a short discussion they decided to use the dove navigational system. After an hour or so the dove came back with just a twig.
'That must be a sign of life,' said Grimbeard.
After a while, the Vikings got to the Celts only to find hundreds of Vikings on the floor, dead!

Chidi Christian Babundo (9)
Benedict House Preparatory School, Sidcup

Tut's Mummy Gets Flushed

King Tut had a pet mummy who was called Daddy. One evening Tut's bodyguard, Hog, accidentally flushed Daddy down the toilet because he thought it was a pile of toilet paper! In those days all the toilets emptied into the River Nile. King Tut was very sad and very mad so he made Hog swim down the River Nile while he sat on his back like he was a boat. Afterwards, they found Daddy and gave him a bath. Then King Tut ordered a feast and they celebrated that Daddy was home. Daddy stayed away from the toilet after that!

Alexander Caseberry (9)
Benedict House Preparatory School, Sidcup

The Great Achievement

'The Germans are coming. They'll finish us. We need to escape,' I said.
'But how?'
'To fire!'
We started shooting the cookie bombs and they went flying towards the Germans. I, John Irving, commander of troops in Trieste, was glad that William Hoskins, a bomb supplier at Woolwich Arsenal, had sent some spies over to transport the cookie bombs, as ours had been stolen by the Germans. One cookie knocked a soldier in the stomach, another went straight into a soldier's mouth. He ate it and the cookie exploded. 'We've done it,' I exclaimed. 'We've defeated the mighty Germans. Hooray!'

Chloe Joyce (9)
Benedict House Preparatory School, Sidcup

Sidd Invents The Wheel

Once upon a time there was a boy called Sidd. Sidd lived with his parents on the River Nile's banks. Sidd's parents had to carry the pharaohs' chair on their shoulders which made them very tired. Sidd was resting under a tree and saw a mouse rolling some twigs into its nest. This gave Sidd an idea. He ran off and told his daddy about it. They both collected logs from the fields. They tied the pharaoh's big chair to the long logs and pulled it around. This made work for people much easier and Sidd had invented the wheel.

Hari Singh Rehal (7)
Benedict House Preparatory School, Sidcup

Battle Of 300

Once there was a bloody war between Sparta and Persia. There were 20,000 Persians and 300 Spartans. This war was Sparta's most epic war because they had 300 Spartans which was the biggest amount of warriors they'd ever had. King Leonidas, the Spartan king, went into the battle and slew and beheaded the Persian warriors. Xerxes, the Persian king, saw the battle whilst sitting on his big, enormous throne, made out of pure, polished, shining gold. He was wearing jewellery everywhere. Xerxes killed all the Spartan warriors. King Leonidas said, 'This is Sparta!' and kicked Xerxes off a high mountain.

Devansh Anand (10)
Benedict House Preparatory School, Sidcup

Slaves And The Pharaoh

One sunny day, Korif and his dad were exploring outside. A man was sneaking up on them, he was the slave-catcher. He caught them in a net and took them to Egypt.
Many days passed and they arrived in Egypt. The slave-catcher brought them to the pharaoh Kafra. 'You will be my slaves,' he said. This frightened Korif so much he fainted.
Korif was now determined to escape from the horrible slave-catcher and Kafra. In the night they snuck out of Egypt to Sudan. 'It's a long way!' said Korif. They had to walk the whole way back to Sudan.

Alfie Moreland (7)
Benedict House Preparatory School, Sidcup

Queen Betty

Once, there lived a princess called Betty. Her mother was Queen Victoria and she had a younger brother, James. James died, then when Betty was eight she had a sister called Mary. When Mary was twenty she started thinking, *Why should Betty be queen?* After that, Mary wanted to become queen and kill Betty. Their mother was getting beheaded in three days so Mary was paying the guards to capture Betty. Mary did not know that her sister knew what her plan was so they put her in the dungeon in the Tower of London. Then Betty became queen.

Tamilore Ekunola (10)
Benedict House Preparatory School, Sidcup

Viking Voyage

A storm hit the longship. It was a gigantic hurricane. Waves were clashing against the wooden sides and leaping over the deck. A hole was ripped out of the rear. It started to sink. The Vikings thought they were going to die. Suddenly, the waves died down and left the ship balanced on a rock.

Two days passed and the sailors were desperate for water to drink. A few of the crew drank seawater and died. The remaining sailors starved to death.

Years later, the explorers found the longship, discovered what had happened and told the world!

Harry Felstead (9)
Benedict House Preparatory School, Sidcup

The Spoilt Mummy

Aya's family were devastated. She was very sick and the doctor said that she didn't have long to live. Aya was only twelve but she was very spoilt. She had so much yet she always wanted more. As soon as Aya died, her funeral preparations took place. Her organs were removed (all except her heart) and she was mummified. Her parents told her that she would have a very expensive and beautiful funeral but Aya was still unhappy. Because of this she haunted her family for the rest of their lives.

Eilish Gavigan (9)
Benedict House Preparatory School, Sidcup

The Berzerkians

The new king, King Harold Bluetooth, was close to tears in his private bedroom. His father had been murdered by a disloyal servant. Now he was the King, but there were many disobedient servants who couldn't be trusted who wanted his throne. He needed a fierce bodyguard who would fear nobody and scare everyone! At that moment, in marched Bert, his top huntsman, sharpening his bloodstained axe. Bert shrieked wildly at Harold's butler who scarpered, terrified. The King now realised it was loyal Bert who would be the head of his new army of powerful, crazy warriors called Berzerkians.

Alfie Murphy (9)
Benedict House Preparatory School, Sidcup

The Challenge!

On one dark, stormy night, the Britons came to the Vikings' village! Now if you didn't know, the Britons were big rivals with the Vikings. The Britons jumped off their boat, went in the village, went to the leader of the Vikings and said that they wanted a challenge and the challenge was to see who could run up the hill the fastest. Whoever won got to keep or swap boats. So Vicki, the leader's daughter, thought fast and gave it to the leader. The leader won and chose to keep their beloved, full-of-gold boat!

Adannam Stephanie Nwokolo (10)
Benedict House Preparatory School, Sidcup

The Tomb Robber!

Once upon a time there was a tomb worker. It was the day before one of the tomb workers was going to mummify Cleopatra but nobody knew that when he mummified Cleopatra he was going to rob her.

Finally the day came and the tomb robber was in action. As soon as he lifted Cleopatra into her tomb, he locked the door but the guards didn't like that he locked the door. Suddenly, the guards caught the tomb robber and put him in pyramid prison for his whole life. Afterwards they got all of Cleopatra's stuff back in her tomb.

Poppy Wakeling (8)
Benedict House Preparatory School, Sidcup

Tooth Fairy Jodie

There is a little girl named Sophia and her tooth has fallen out. Luckily Jodie is the right tooth fairy to take Sophia's tooth and leave her a present behind.

Outside Sophia's window it's cold and windy but thankfully Jodie is ready to sneak through to Sophia's bedroom.

As Jodie creeps in, she slowly snuggles underneath Sophia's pillow to find her tooth. She receives it and leaves a charm bracelet behind.

The next morning, Sophia slowly feels under her pillow and finds the bracelet. She's so surprised and happy though, that she runs down the stairs to show her parents.

Brooke Blair (10)
Benedict House Preparatory School, Sidcup

The Curse Of Tut's Tomb

After years of looking for Tut's tomb in Ancient Egypt, an archaeologist called Carter discovered it. He sent a letter to his friend Carnarvon in England because he was paying for the tomb to be dug up. When Carnarvon arrived, the tomb was dug up and he entered it.

One morning, when Carnarvon was shaving, a mosquito bit him and he became very ill. He had a high fever and chills and died. At the exact time he died, all the lights in Cairo mysteriously went out. Now everyone is afraid to enter Tut's cursed tomb!

Kiara Bwanandeke (7)
Benedict House Preparatory School, Sidcup

At The Roman Bath

Marco (a rich Roman man) went to his favourite place, the Roman baths. He loved to go there so he could relax while making new friends. His slave covered him with oil to wash him while he was chatting to a new friend, Nicholas, who was as rich as he was. They started to talk about life. Unexpectedly, they began to argue about who was richer and who had more slaves and power. They started to kick and punch each other but kept slipping since they were covered in oil. They started to laugh and became best friends forever.

Alessio Bassan (9)
Benedict House Preparatory School, Sidcup

An Old Sea War!

The Caribbean Sea, so peaceful, calm - *bang!* Oh yeah, apart from the pirates of course and the Nepolians.
'Can you keep it down, I'm trying to write a mini saga here!...'
'Use all of the gunpowder men, give them the taste rum,' said Captain Swashbuckle, with a harsh grin.
Meanwhile, on the other ship... 'Filthy pirates, they'll soon know who's boss,' said Ramses III (captain of the Nepolians).
They fought ferociously, you couldn't know who was winning. Then the pirates made a hole in their ship! The last cannon fired and the last lives were taken by the pirates.

Dhanvin Vinothkumar (9)
Benedict House Preparatory School, Sidcup

Blue Beard

'Are you mad, Captain?'

'Why?'

'Well the Musketeers stole our biscuit treasure and they're eating it right now.'

'Maybe we are in for a stroke of luck. The Musketeers aren't too far ahead of us!'

'Captain Stealer, stop right there! Give us our treasure back!'

'Your treasure?'

'Wait a second, Captain Stealer, who are these?'

'New, trained crew mates of mine from the real world!'

'Hey! New Musketeers, join my team and I'll give you the biggest TV in the world.'

'But I'll give you the sharpest swords in the world.'

'Well I'll let you have unlimited biscuits.'

'We're in!'

Arjan Thind (9)
Benedict House Preparatory School, Sidcup

When Right Turns Wrong

'My plan is perfect!'

James (who was one of my friends) asked, 'What is your plan again?'

'Seriously, you should have been listening! Okay, so the plan is we get the explosives from the shed and put cord in Parliament. Steve and Jack will be doing that and James and I will wait for you two here next to the pond. Then we can see the beautiful fireworks.'

Later that night, we were just about to start the plan but the guards found us and we were in jail for years.

Zahra Ashby (11)
Benenden CE Primary School, Cranbrook

The Nightmare

In the mist of the blue sea, I saw the outlines of Viking longboats heading towards our shores. The atmosphere changed. We had heard so much about the Vikings although I wish I hadn't; just the thought of fearless warriors who fought until their deaths with pride was bad enough, but this was like a living nightmare. We all ran, leaving our treasures behind in hope we would get away. I could hear babies scream, their parents captured and taken for slavery. Sadly I was the sole survivor.

Nico Doane (11)
Benenden CE Primary School, Cranbrook

Vikings

It was a nice morning to get in our monastery. I didn't know what to do. I was terrified. I told the other monks. I tried to stop them but I couldn't. I tried with all my might, I really couldn't stop them. I told the other monks but they were dead. One had a sword in his eye and his head. I didn't think they liked us very much. They were not very nice. I would do anything for them to go away as they were really mean. What could I do...?

Kiera Ashton
Benenden CE Primary School, Cranbrook

Dreaded Day

I woke up in a jolly mood this morning. I felt so exhilarated. John and James were in the chapel downstairs. I went down there to greet them. Suddenly, there were three ear-shattering knocks on the door. I really didn't want to get up because I was concentrating on my writing. Then the door was knocked down with a massive boom; five ferocious Vikings were standing in the doorway. Despite their scary appearance, I didn't lose faith in myself. They stormed through the chapel and then started the slaughtering...

Olivia Bo Hazelwood (11)
Benenden CE Primary School, Cranbrook

The Raiding At Lindisfarne

I could see longships in the distance. I'd never seen these ones before. When they arrived we could see they were fully armed. I asked a few men to help me barricade the wall. We could hear them charging up the hill. The huge men thumped on the door and started shouting blood-curdling screeches. When we didn't let them in they started knocking the wall down. When they had got through, we called for the men to get the weapons. We knew how to fight, but they beat us to the ground. They stole our slaves, women and treasure.

Ben Ansell (11)
Benenden CE Primary School, Cranbrook

Don't Lose Your Head!

'Have you heard the news?'
'Yes, I can't believe Henry beheaded his wife!'
'I just feel really sorry for her. She didn't do anything wrong. She wouldn't dare to.'
'Henry is such a tyrant!'
'Rumours are that he's met his third wife already!'
'Poor Anne, how dreadful to be locked in the dank, dismal Tower of London, knowing what her fate will be!'
'Maybe Henry does have a heart. He did hire that French swordsman, which must have made a dent in his riches!'
'Let's hope her poor daughter, Elizabeth, doesn't meet the same fate!'

Zoe Daverson (10)
Benenden CE Primary School, Cranbrook

The Old Chimney

Yet again he made me clean the sooty chimney; it was so full today. I was really struggling to breathe through my scarred lungs. My elbows were really grazed and sore, they were actually starting to bleed. When the day was over I went to the shop since I had just got my pay, so I got some milk. Then I lay down in the shelter of the dirty, trampled street, but it was better than nothing. One of the downsides was that it was a grey and stormy day.

Bluebelle Hawker (11)
Benenden CE Primary School, Cranbrook

Poppies

Cries of anger, hatred and woe fill my ears. Pink rays of sun shower the countryside, darkness is falling. Gunshots pierce the air around us, landing in the hearts of innocent men. Friends and foe fall gracefully to the ground, silenced for evermore... I plead for mercy, the gentle breeze sways the poppies to and fro. My soul is empty. I want to weep for my fellow soldiers, how brave and strong, but now my life has been sucked out of existence. So here I lie in Flanders Fields.

Amelia Madeleine Thomas (11)
Benenden CE Primary School, Cranbrook

Chaos

Help! It's the end. I know it is. This has happened before, but it's different! All my pots are smashing, like a mirror with no hope. Help! I'm panicking! My two daughters can't die. They're only babies, not middle-aged women! Oh no, the volcano has started to speak. I always knew Vesuvius was sleeping. Everyone is screaming; they're screaming blood-curdling screams. Stay positive! Don't freak. Just be grateful for what you have. Help! The end is nigh... I'm clenching my daughters in my scalding, sweaty arms...

Edie Colquhoun (11)
Benenden CE Primary School, Cranbrook

Pompeii Peril

It was a hot day in the city of Pompeii. All was calm and the citizens were getting on with their jobs. However, the volcano was moaning and groaning, almost as if it was in pain. The citizens thought it was nothing so they carried on... Suddenly, the side of the mountain blew off and scorching-hot gas rushed down, it was heading to the city and destroying everything in its path! Would this be the end?

Stanley Brothers (11)
Benenden CE Primary School, Cranbrook

Theseus And The Minotaur

Theseus was furious about all of the people being killed by the son, the Minotaur. He decided to sneak onto the boat full of people to be sacrificed for the Minotaur. After many hours on board, Theseus finally arrived on the Minotaur's island. With a stolen sword, he crept to the cave's entrance, where he met the king's daughter. She gave him string to tie to the gate, so he could find his way out. He entered the cave and felt a breath on the back of his neck...

Travis Orton (10)
Brookland CE Primary School, Romney Marsh

The Tomb

The sand was warm on my feet. Being brave, I stepped into the darkness of the tomb. Suddenly, there was a spine-thrilling chill; it gave me a cold shiver. I moved further away from the entrance however, as I did, I saw a booby trap. At first I froze with shock, but then swiftly I ran. As I sped for safety, I stumbled across an entrance so I ventured in. There, on the floor, lay heaps of glimmering gold. It shone like the sun setting.

Ruby Jackman (9)
Brookland CE Primary School, Romney Marsh

Joseph Mengele's Day At The Camps

On this dark, gloomy day, Joseph was choosing between slavery and death; although millions upon millions hated Josef Mengele. Josef was Hitler's most respected soldier. While he loved his ruler, he did have a personal life. During WWII, when at work, he wouldn't quit his job unless his life depended on it. He was in control of camps, soldiers and a tonne of military equipment, so there were many who were afraid of him. He was known as a dangerous, horrific man. One day he was pronounced dead and was never seen again.

Ben Maka Chantler (10)
Brookland CE Primary School, Romney Marsh

The Great Trip To Egypt

It all started in 3000 BC. An explorer walked into the ancient pyramid. He went into the room and saw five (very well-decorated) tombs. Suddenly, the first tomb in the row opened, a mummy peered its head out. The explorer roared a high-pitched scream, 'Argh!' and ran down some stairs. He hid behind another tomb.
As always, it opened and a little girl came crawling out with her kitten. She said, 'We'd better run, it's coming,'
The little girl's kitten gave a small miaow.
'Who's coming then?'
They turned and saw it was already there, they were shocked...

Olivia Blackman (9)
Brookland CE Primary School, Romney Marsh

19

Deeds, Not Words

I was told to say a speech to the suffragettes today. I walked into the town hall, 'Hello everyone, we have a new member. I'll tell her how I became a suffragette. I worked in a washing service; I received five shillings while men got ten. One day I thought, *Why live in the men's shadows?* So I made the suffragettes. My mother died because we only had five shillings to buy food. I will tell you a secret: my father supported all of us. We all need to know the fight is far from over.'

Anna Bowden (10)
Brookland CE Primary School, Romney Marsh

The Dark Horse

It felt like hours waiting in the scorching heat, in the dark, in silence. It was unbearable. Suddenly, we started moving, there was only one place we could be going to (the city). All we heard was the cheering and celebrating of the people. We heard the king shout, 'We've won, they've given up. The siege is over.' 'When do we attack?' whispered the colonel.
I replied, 'We'll attack when the city is asleep.'
As the clock struck 12, we crept out of the wooden horse, but suddenly the alarm resounded. I shouted, 'Attack! We must rescue Helen!'

Maggie Hick (11)
Brookland CE Primary School, Romney Marsh

Days In The Factory

It was an ordinary day, placing dynamite in boxes. All of a sudden, a noise came from downstairs... the explosion had been set off. Questions were racing through my head. *Is everyone OK? Will I be OK?*
Pounding on the factory door was the police, shouting, 'Evacuate the building!'
I couldn't get out, they wouldn't allow me. I was pleading for help, no one replied. All around me were crying children shouting, 'Mum, Dad, help!' Some were dying from the fumes coming from the fire, others were struggling to breathe. What could I do?

Charlie Jackman (11)
Brookland CE Primary School, Romney Marsh

The Mummy

Sand was brushing against my feet. I dug down to see if anything was below. Suddenly, I came across a tomb. I became curious so I had a peek inside. Next thing I knew, I was being chased by a cursed mummy! I tried to escape but unfortunately the mummy was standing on my shadow. Sadly, I came to a dead end and leant on the back wall... It opened. I found a chest so I looked inside: there was a whip. As the mummy was getting close, I whipped the mummy and returned it to its tomb.

Maddie Dean (9)
Brookland CE Primary School, Romney Marsh

Perseus And Medusa's Head

Battling the waves, we made it to the cave where Medusa lurked. Slowly, I entered her territory. Clutching my sword, I walked on. Glancing at the statues, I heard a voice, 'I sense you, today will be your last.'
Walking carefully into a secret path, I found myself on the other side: where Medusa was standing! I swiftly chopped off her head, grabbed it and escaped the cave. Without looking back, I leapt back onto the boat and sailed back home. I couldn't wait to tell everyone the exciting news.

Emilie Haines (10)
Brookland CE Primary School, Romney Marsh

A Strange New World

Viciously, the storm battered the hull of the ship. Huge waves swept over the wooden floorboard. A torrent of wind blew wildly; the gust flew freely through the ship. It was as cold as ice. Suddenly, a floorboard came loose and flew towards me. Before long, I was unconscious. Beside me, a fire roared like a lion which seemed to pounce in my direction.
I slowly gained my vision and saw that I was near the wreckage of the boat.
'Come on Captain, we need to move,' my first mate explained.
'Where are we?' I replied inquisitively.
'The New World.'

Luke Stenings (10)
Brookland CE Primary School, Romney Marsh

Empty-Handed

In a panic, I leapt out of the leather boat seat and cried, 'We only have exactly one hour to find the perfect jewel for Queen Victoria's tiara and we still haven't found out where we can find it!' Rushing, we finally came to a small Island.

'Quick! We need to locate one in time for the wedding!' the second Victorian inventor explained.

We hopped off the boat onto the shore. Although we had been working for hours, we were empty-handed.

When we arrived home, Queen Victoria was furious.

'What happened, you two?' she screamed. 'Send them to the dungeon!'

Ella Price (9)
Brookland CE Primary School, Romney Marsh

World War Boom

Watching the last British planes fall out of the skies, the final carrier plane, loaded with bombs, headed for the field, ready to drop them. As he was about to descend, deadly missiles were being fired. The pilot dodged them, until the tail was shot!

'Mayday!' shouted the pilot. 'I'm badly hit, I'm going down!' The plane was losing altitude fast. He tried to keep the plane in the air but it was no use; he was going to crash. He collided into a German bunker. All was black...

England had won! 'God save our king.'

Kai David Dean (10)
Brookland CE Primary School, Romney Marsh

The Ruby War

Daphne and Velma flew to ancient Egypt and right behind them was evil Mr Creek.
Daphne saw him slide into a pyramid, so they slid after him.
Unfortunately, they both fell in different holes filled with treasures. In the first, there was a map to where the ruby was hidden. Creek managed to find the two teenagers and reached for the map...
'What are you doing?' screamed Daphne.
'I need that map!' Creek exclaimed.
'No!' shouted Velma. They both went to find the ruby. Finally, they'd found it...
'Let's destroy it,' Velma suggested.
'Let's do it,' Daphne agreed.

Jasmine J Bull (10)
Brookland CE Primary School, Romney Marsh

65 Million Years Ago

'Hello?' called Jay, but nobody answered. Suddenly, there was a deafening scream and then a crunch. Jay was sweating as he turned around... 'Argh!' Jay hit the floor, struggling for survival. What had pounced on him was beyond belief, a raptor! He was in a forest 65 million years ago, with dinosaurs! He daren't think of what the scream and crunch was, so he kicked at the raptor, rolled away and sprinted for his life!
Amazingly, he had lost the raptor, which was extremely unusual because they were very fast. Climbing up a tree, Jay felt much safer...

Joseph Edmed (10)
Brookland CE Primary School, Romney Marsh

The Death

Horror was all around me, from rats and bodies to some quacks trying to save lives. Suddenly, my neighbour stumbled through his door past the painted 'red cross' and fell to my feet. In terror, I ran the furthest I could until my chest became tight and I felt dizzy. Coughing, I put my hand to my mouth, only to see blood. As my eyes slowly closed, I knew this was it. The Black Death had got me at last. I fell to the ground with a thump and my vision faded.

Jack Blackman (11)
Brookland CE Primary School, Romney Marsh

The Egyptian Mummy Who Wanted A Child

It all started in 3000 BC. A mummy lay there, in a pyramid. She wasn't just an ordinary mummy. She was one who always got confused.
One scorching day, she awakened and wondered, *Mummies have children...* So she opened her tomb, escaped from the pyramid and fled to find a child!
Down in the sandy village, people ran from the mummy, screaming! Finally, just one little girl was left. The mummy grabbed her and scattered home to her tomb.
She didn't know she was an Egyptian mummy, not a human mummy. When she woke up, it was just a dream.

Kailash Davy (10)
Brookland CE Primary School, Romney Marsh

Evacuated

It was a cold, misty morning and I gazed around looking for my mum. I was separated from my family because of war. My teacher took us out and we trudged to the nearest train station. Then we were given postcards and forced to write to our family. We were OK. The antique train was as dirty as an abandoned house. As the train moved I got up and waved to my mother, however she didn't catch my attention. Then the train stopped. I came out and looked around. What would happen to me?

Isaac Olajide (10)
Burnt Oak Primary School, Gillingham

Stonehenge

One day I went to Stonehenge. We walked through the storm. Finally we were there. It was amazing to see Stonehenge, it was the best time of my life because I have never gone to Stonehenge. I got to sit on rocks and all of my family were with me and my friends, it was the best day ever. Suddenly, the storm got worse and I nearly got blown over. I was really scared but I had to get home. I didn't know if we were going to make it but we did.

Courtney Irwin (8)
Burnt Oak Primary School, Gillingham

Illuminati Pyramid

In ancient Egyptian time there was a young boy called Nandos, he loved awesome adventures.

One day he found a temple in the middle of nowhere so he entered. He didn't know it was cursed by the Illuminati. Triangles were everywhere but one had an eye, then it said, 'Let me eat you!'

He then fell into a trap to be mummified. The triangles there took out all of his organs and stuffed them into jars, he screamed louder than an elephant but died and never returned.

Joshua Tyrone (10)
Burnt Oak Primary School, Gillingham

The Obliteration

Splash! 'Man overboard!' the captain of the English ship shouted. Suddenly, the enemy's boat appeared. Out of the corner of my eye I spotted them reloading a brutal cannon. Before I knew it, *boom!* The ship began to sink.

'Argh!' screamed everyone.

The soldiers of the English ship fought to their last breaths under the ice-cold water, while swiftly the brutal assassin from the German ship climbed the flag pole and shot his enemies one by one - *bang!*

Tyler Woollett (10)
Burnt Oak Primary School, Gillingham

Untitled

'All aboard!' said the conductor as he got on the train. My sister started to cry because she couldn't say goodbye to our mum. I picked my brother and sister up and went on the train. Once we were on the train, my sister said that it stunk like a skunk. My brother used his T-shirt to cover his nose and said, 'When are we going to go home?'
I told him that we would be home by Christmas Day to make them feel better. This has been the worst day of my life so far.

Kenzly Wells (9)
Burnt Oak Primary School, Gillingham

The Lucky Evacuee

Long ago there lived a girl called Kathleen. She was an evacuee of WWII. Obviously she had to leave her parents and she was terrified. Although she didn't mind leaving her dad because he was bad. When she arrived at the countryside she had to *live* with a woman called Miss McBride. She was very nice to Kathleen. However, she didn't cook very well. Miss McBride took Kathleen to a bakery and she could pick out anything. She picked a vanilla cream then she saw a bomb. Luckily it didn't hit her.

Hallee Wells (9)
Burnt Oak Primary School, Gillingham

Florence Nightingale

When Florence Nightingale was a little girl, she was eager to be a lantern-carrying, helpful nurse. Florence grew up to be a nurse and her ladies travelled to the Crimean War so they could help the soldiers to get better. The soldiers thought Florence was the best nurse in the world.

Shania Stone (8)
Burnt Oak Primary School, Gillingham

Dear Diary

Dear Diary, I've just arrived in Gillingham. It was a horrendous journey. I had to go on a slow, rusty train. Luckily, I wasn't the only one. When I got there, there were loads of men with belts to whip us and make us get in a stinky, dirty cow pen so people could look at us. It reminded me of my annoying, mean mum at home. She used to whip me with a belt even though I had done nothing wrong. Someone finally chose me and put me in a really nice home. I'm still really sad though.

Bobby Brinn (9)
Burnt Oak Primary School, Gillingham

The Attack

'Pilot, there's a ship ahead. You must attack!' Captain Dykes said. The pilot quickly changed direction and headed towards the enemy ship. The waves crashed and water spat onto the ship. *Boom!* The gigantic boat was on its way. Quickly, Captain Dykes unleashed at the enemy and fired a large cannon ball straight at them. *Crash! Boom!* The ship exploded into pieces and sunk down to the bottom of the sea. 'Hooray,' shouted the captain. Suddenly, the allies' ship was targeted too. The pilot rapidly chased the enemy plane to eliminate them. Bombs flew across the dark, miserable sky.

Faith Julie Ann Dykes (11)
Burnt Oak Primary School, Gillingham

The Evacuee

'Okay, I think that's everyone on now.' We all sat silently on the stinky train wondering what to say or do. I honestly didn't know where we were even going. I asked a boy next to me and he said we were going to a village because World War Two was starting. I panicked inside wondering why this tragedy would happen. I started to cry a lot with fear. The train stopped really fast, everyone got off. As I got off the train I bumped into a boy, he was going home with the same lady as me. Phew!

Paris Purdue (10)
Burnt Oak Primary School, Gillingham

The Death Of Tutankhamun

One beautiful, sunny day, Tutankhamun was baking some bread for dinner. Tutankhamun went fishing in the Red Sea. Tutankhamun knew there were snakes such as cobras.
The next day he went back fishing, but this time in the River Nile. Suddenly, a cobra swallowed Tutankhamun whole. All of Tut's friends tried to get him out but they could not get him out. They mummified the snake with Tut inside. When his brother found out, he crowned himself.
The next day, all of Tut's slaves took all of his valuables and other stuff to his tomb. It was very sad.

Joeb Church (8)
Burnt Oak Primary School, Gillingham

The Marriage

Long ago, in the land of the ancient Egyptians, was a young king named Tutankhamun. He was getting ready for his wonderful wedding to marry Ankhesenamun. Ra, the sun god, announced that tomorrow morning the wedding would take place. King Tutankhamun and Ankhesenamun invited the whole of Egypt except the horrible people.
The next morning there was panic, King Tut got into his luxury gold outfit with a lapis lazuli chin cone while Ankhesenamun got into her luxury quartz dress. She walked down the red velvet aisle. The crowd went wild. Happily, the couple got married.

Alfie Delaney Dugard (10)
Burnt Oak Primary School, Gillingham

An Exciting Discovery

One week ago there was a king that was living a happy life, but two days later he died. His pretty sister and his ugly brother were trying to discover Tutankhamun's tomb. Luckily, Howard Carter was there to help them. Did you know that Howard Carter and his friends actually discovered Tutankhamun's tomb? Tutankhamun's brother and sister were feeling worried as they were seeing their brother's body.

One day later, Howard Carter said, 'We could go to the church.' They agreed.

If Tutankhamun was still alive now he would be seeing what we can now see.

Sophia Watkins (8)
Burnt Oak Primary School, Gillingham

John's Diary

Dear Diary, It has now been a week in this terrible place. It smells like horse poop and my friend is dead. However, they don't know that there's someone coming for me. He is a random man I saw on the streets who is feeding me. The good thing is that he is an English soldier in disguise. Secretly, he stuffs a pierce of tissue down the drain of my cell. I hope tomorrow will be a better day for me and I will manage to escape.

Maddison Turner (9)
Burnt Oak Primary School, Gillingham

How Cleopatra Died

Cleopatra was the last pharaoh. She was as radiant as a rose petal. She loved Julius Caesar. They wanted to unite their countries. Alexander found out that Caesar liked Cleopatra and felt betrayed; so he told the Greeks that he was a betrayer. They went to war with Caesar, he did not survive the war and died. When sad Cleopatra found out, she began to get really stressed out and didn't know what to do, so she got a deadly snake and killed herself with it. The snake's teeth were as sharp as jagged ice. Slowly she fell.

Emmanuella Ikwetie (9)
Burnt Oak Primary School, Gillingham

The Evacuation

Dear Diary, 'Come on,' yelled the man. 'It is time to go on the train.'
The children hurried to get on the train. The train was stinky, smelly, old and it had no toilets. I saw a girl wearing a pink ragged frock and blue shoes. She was crying because she got separated from her mum. She was sitting next to a boy and the boy said, 'Don't cry, you will be back by Christmas.'
'Where are we going?' said the girl.
'We are going to stay at somebody's house.'

Adelina Bajrami (9)
Burnt Oak Primary School, Gillingham

Tutankhamun Battle

One day there was a brave man called Tutankhamun. One evening he went to battle. Later that day, he camped for the night. The pharaoh heard a horrible noise coming from outside. Tutankhamun woke up and said, 'What is that noise?'
The guards turned up with four army people. They said, 'We want to join your group.'
'Yes,' he said so they marched to Hitler.
When they got there, they opened the door quickly but there stood the whole Hitler Army. Tutankhamun was angry at the two strangers and single-handedly slew the army. Egypt won again.

Nicole Worship (9)
Burnt Oak Primary School, Gillingham

The Hoplite

Long ago, in the land of ancient Greece, there was a fierce hoplite that went into a gruesome and brutal battle in the scorching-hot sun with sweat dripping down his back. First, the hoplites grabbed their bows and arrows and fired arrows with sharp tips that glistened in the sunlight. The Athenians quickly grabbed their shields and protected their scared faces. After that the scary Spartan king chucked a shiny spear into a warrior's head and blood splattered out the poor guy's head like a water pipe split open. The Spartans charged and obliterated Athens and they were defeated.

Johnny Harbard (9)
Burnt Oak Primary School, Gillingham

How The King Died

One day King Tut was in the kitchen, shouting at his cook for making horrible food. This made the cook very angry. It was payback time. Later on that day, King Tut went out hunting. It was time for the cook to make dinner. He made delicious lasagne and added one last touch, it was poison! Then the king came back and brought a lion to eat tomorrow but was there gonna be a tomorrow? He tasted it. It was now time for the main part. The cook evilly smiled and, in a second, the king was lifeless.

Zaina Khan (9)
Burnt Oak Primary School, Gillingham

Smutt The Caveman

'Why are you here?' Smutt asked Danny Diplodcus.
'I'm here because I live here, Danny,' replied Smutt. Smutt lived in a new £1,000 cave. In addition it came fully furnished with a stone, charcoal-powered stove and a comfy leaf bed.
Danny was Smutt's best friend but also a deadly enemy because he was a dinosaur. Smutt asked Danny to dinner when, suddenly... Smutt stuck his crystal spear into Danny! Smutt dragged Danny to his spit roast and added some lavender. Smutt's spear was all bloody. Just as Danny was ready, two young pterodactyls took Danny to their high home...

Ellie Prebble (10)
Burnt Oak Primary School, Gillingham

The Discovery Of Greece!

One day there were two brave and mighty treasure hunters who were always finding treasure. The treasure hunters, Max and Jackson, found out about Ancient Greek treasure in a massive cave. Suddenly, they went out of the house and went to find the treasure.

Two hours later they had to cross the ocean, luckily they'd brought a boat. As they were crossing the ocean they saw Poseidon, the god of the sea. They finally got past the ocean and got to the lake. The treasure was all gold with some epic and cool silver statues.

Max Piper (8)
Burnt Oak Primary School, Gillingham

Collision

'Man that station!' cried Zeus.

'They're coming,' screeched Poseidon.

The gods got prepared for battle against Hades and his demons. 'I'm hit,' bellowed Hermes.

Thunder roared and lightning crashed, the wind soared and the rain zapped and Hades yelled, 'Attack!'

Zeus hurled bolts, Poseidon fought with his powerful trident but they were too strong. Eventually Hades captured the gods one by one, until only one was left. 'This is horrific! I'm the only one left. I need assistance,' murmured Hercules. 'I must set off to find Aphrodite, goddess of love,' shouted Hercules proudly.

Keelan Philpott (10)
Burnt Oak Primary School, Gillingham

Roman Disaster

Long ago, in a popular town called Popular Circle, the Romans had the whole world under their feet. Romans had control of all the poor people and rich, wealthy people. The Celts grew jealous. They wanted the world in their hands so they had a sneaky plan. It was to prank the Romans. It was going to be epic. The pranks were making wine into blood and having a noisy night with terrible food. The Romans were defeated and it was soon better with the Celts in charge. Wait, the Celts were mean! What were they going to do?

Eve Hooper (9)
Burnt Oak Primary School, Gillingham

Kayla's First Experience!

Beep, beep!
'Quick, to the Anderson shelter outside in the playground - quick, quick, quick!' screamed Miss Stergeon, panicking due to the fact that the siren was unexpected, also because it was the first one ever.
'Waa, I'm scared. I want my mummy!' cried Kayla, a three-year-old schoolgirl.
Miss Stergeon calmed her down and gave her a warm cup of tea.
Bang! A German plane fell to the floor with a loud bang.
'Britain has won the First World War, let's celebrate!'
They threw a huge party to celebrate their victory against Germany.
'We've won. Yeah!'

Shana Poole
Burnt Oak Primary School, Gillingham

The Wrong King

One day Tutankhamun travelled to the desert. He dropped his sword, climbed off his chariot and picked up his sword. Suddenly, a rattlesnake came slithering up to him. Then it bit him. He fainted and he went pale. A few minutes later he awoke and got on his chariot and went home.

The next day he passed away after breakfast. Everyone was devastated when they heard that he'd passed away. His brother found out and was happy but sad at the same time. He was happy because he could be king. He was sad because taking over wasn't right.

Kristen Woolley (9)
Burnt Oak Primary School, Gillingham

The Evacuees

Dear Diary, It was a cold and windy day when I had to go to the countryside because we were getting bombed. I went on a train with all my luggage. I muttered, 'Bye Mum,' and waved and we went off.

We got off the train and we got taken to wherever this woman took us. I got taken to this old man, to me he looked like he was grumpy. He asked if I wanted to come in so I walked in and asked if I could eat something. He seemed nice.

Katlyn Savage (10)
Burnt Oak Primary School, Gillingham

The Making Of Electricity!

There was once a blacksmith who lived in Rome. Her name was Boudicca. She was a diligent and easy-going lady. One day, she was under the rain holding a wooden bowl. Lightning struck the bowl. The electricity slithered up her skin. She got shocked. After four weeks, the citizens hadn't noticed Boudicca. She rose up. Anything she touched electrified, therefore she killed nine people. She found out she had electric powers and named it Electricity. She started using it as a blacksmith and soon discovered she was able to control her powers and use them for good.

Janice Ighauodha (8)
Burnt Oak Primary School, Gillingham

The Ancient Lizard

A long time ago there was a country called Egypt, the hottest country you would ever see or feel. The rarest animal in Egypt was a lizard named Gecko but this lizard wasn't just any lizard, it was a lonely, kind lizard.
The very sad thing about the lizard was it got bullied every day. Gecko the lizard told his mum and his teachers but it was no use. One day Gecko went to climb the biggest pyramid when, suddenly, he fell off. Luckily the bullies caught him and they were friends forever.

Jasmine White (10)
Burnt Oak Primary School, Gillingham

Untitled

Centuries ago there was a strong, fierce dinosaur, Roar. He had a friend named Scratch. He was scared of everything. One day, the volcano erupted. Gloomy smoke shot from the volcano. Roar had a brilliant idea. He said, 'We need to stop the volcano, let's climb up.'
Scratch didn't agree. Slowly but carefully they clambered up the volcano. Scratch climbed on the top but lost his balance and fell in. Roar peered over and scanned the area and, out the corner of his eye, he spotted Scratch and pulled him up. As he did, the volcano slowly stopped erupting.

Saphanya Philpott (9)
Burnt Oak Primary School, Gillingham

Egyptian Mess

One scorching-hot day, Cassie and Sadie got out of their Egyptian huts. They strolled to the pyramids and took a look inside. They started to explore and came to a room.
They walked inside and saw two ghosts, Cleopatra and Tutankhamun. They got out the pyramid to get revenge on Tut's brother.
They persuaded them both not to kill Tut's brother so Cleo and Tut went back to the pyramid to sleep for one million years. Then Cassie and Sadie walked back home.

Raiah Russell-Heard (10)
Burnt Oak Primary School, Gillingham

Indominus Rex

Millions of years ago, in the Jurassic period, deep in the jungle a T-rex was hunting for raptors when a raptor found him. It was a lonely raptor and they became friends and had many adventures. Unfortunately, dark forces had awoken, creating a beast of terror called the Indominus rex. He was hungry for world domination and the world's only hope was Remix and Rerx. The mighty creature made its way through the forest, destroying everything that moved, until he found them and fought with great strength. However they were too late. He went super crazy and the beast succeeded.

Alfie Hatcher (9)
Burnt Oak Primary School, Gillingham

The Snake Who Found His Smile

As the sun was shining and the sun was glimmering like gold, Shychack the snake was slithering down sandy hills all alone.
'Oh I wish I had a marvellous smile,' he moaned.
As he slithered on, he met his pal Nalu, the camel.
'Why are you always unhappy?' she asked.
'I don't have any friends,' he cried.
'Yes you do,' she replied and walked away.
The snake slithered away for a week and a day and still felt very lonely. When he saw a puddle, it showed his reflection. Then he knew that there was someone with him: his smile.

Tracy Lartey (9)
Burnt Oak Primary School, Gillingham

Boudicca's Not-So-Brilliant Battle

Long ago, in the time of the Celts, Boudicca's parents gave birth to Boudicca. As time went on, Boudicca got in the habit of becoming a farmer. Boudicca was soon an excellent farmer.
'Please could you harvest my crops?' asked a lady.
'Oh sure,' replied Boudicca.
After a few weeks, Boudicca accidentally ruined the lady's crops.
'Caesar, attack!' screamed the lady.
'You can never beat us,' shouted the leader. *Bang!*
'I, Boudicca, vow to kill you.' *Bang!*
'I surrender, you have killed everybody I love.'
Boudicca will always be remembered for her determination and bravery.

Yajna Rungien
Burnt Oak Primary School, Gillingham

Untitled

I was walking down the road. There was a girl, her purse got taken because a man took the purse. I ran down the road and the lady got the purse back. I pinned him to the floor like the police.
'Thank you!' she said.
'I don't want money,' I replied. Then I went home. I was a hero.

Ryan Jay Hart (10)
Burnt Oak Primary School, Gillingham

The Story Of Stonehenge

One day, I saw strong men with big rocks and they were building Stonehenge. They took ages to build Stonehenge. When I was eight years old, they only needed little stones and it took centuries. Then they all had to go to other countries to find little stones. They then found one little stone. Soon after they found lots more. They had to build the rest of Stonehenge and it took five years to finish putting in all of the little stones. There were thousands of people at Stonehenge and this is how it was made.

Jake Moseley (8)
Burnt Oak Primary School, Gillingham

Egyptians

'Hurry up with that statue. Your life depends on it!' *Boom!* 'Be careful with that statue, that is my most treasured thing ever apart from Cleopatra.'
'Sorry King Tutankhamun, I won't do it again.'
'Hello Daddy,' said Cleopatra.
'Hey, nobody move. Tutankhamum give me your daughter or else!' yelled the imposter.
'Okay, bye Cleo.'
'Now let me be king or I'll whip her.'
'Never!'
'Okay, have it your way.' - *Whip whip whip!*
'My daughter's dead. Now where's the tomb? I'll carry her.' *Plop!*
'Now time to put her in the cave. I will miss you.'

Danielle Cole (10)
Burnt Oak Primary School, Gillingham

Vanished

Yesterday I was strolling through the forest when, suddenly, I discovered a pedestal so I chucked my bag on it. Then, mysteriously, the floor curiously collapsed and I fell into a mysterious land full of genies. It was full of everyone's wishes. It was metal. I discovered a genie that wasn't already used so I made a wish to be like Goliath. Suddenly, I got vanished into a volcano. I jumped in and saved a man so I got vanished again, back to my world. I was strong like John Cena. I was very crazy.

Calum Groot (9)
Burnt Oak Primary School, Gillingham

Untitled

In ancient Greek times there lived a man who considered himself the fastest in the world.
One day, he entered the first Olympic Games. He entered all of the events.
Four days later, Om-Bolt had missed three of the events as he had been fast asleep.
The last event was about to begin. He arrived just in the nick of time but was out of breath from the running. He watched the other runners disappear into the distance. He tried to catch up with them but unfortunately he lost the race.
'Maybe I'm not the fastest in the world.'

Jayden Taylor-Harding (9)
Burnt Oak Primary School, Gillingham

Cereal Animals

One morning, I woke up and I went to have breakfast. Suddenly, the animals in my cereal box came to life! There was a tiger, monkey and chicken rampaging through my kitchen. So I shut the door so my mother couldn't hear them. Surprisingly, my future self appeared and gave me a formula to put them back into their boxes! I poured it on them and it transformed them into their boxes. It was the best day of my life! I met the animals in my cereal in real life! I would never forget this outstanding, glorious day.

Keana Roxanne Melo (9)
Burnt Oak Primary School, Gillingham

The Stonehenge Adventure

Once there were five kids that lived in Stonehenge and they killed animals for food. One dark night, a wolf army came and broke Stonehenge. Jake said, 'Our house is gone, let's go!'
Everyone left Stonehenge.
Five years later, they had made axes and they chopped down trees and used the wood to make houses. The five kids made all the things they needed. Whenever the wolf army came, they fought back so all their houses would never break again.

Taylor Bullas (7)
Burnt Oak Primary School, Gillingham

The Day Of Luck

One day, a girl called Carly was taking a stroll down the park
when she fell in a gigantic, prickly bush and fell into a coma.
Soon after, Carly woke up and found herself in a mystical land.
A lucky unicorn appeared in front of her eyes. After a while, the
unicorn started to speak, 'Young one, I shall give you a wish.'
Carly replied, 'I only wish for luck.'
The unicorn's horn started to glow and then the unicorn vanished.
One hour later, Carly was pushed off a cliff but was saved by a
bouncy trampoline.

Molly Bailey (9)
Burnt Oak Primary School, Gillingham

Stonehenge

The day was going quickly, I was at home and my parents asked,
'Can you go and put the last stone on?'
'Seriously?'
'Yes,'
'My pleasure.'
I went to Stonehenge and I put the last stone on, it was amazing.
It felt great to do it so I went home and I had my lunch. My
parents went to see the sun on the rocks and it was lovely.

Inês Henriques (8)
Burnt Oak Primary School, Gillingham

Animal Attack

One day, I awoke to find myself face-to-face with a terrifying baboon. I hoped it was just a bad dream but it wasn't. I was in a jungle. I ran away from it. It was a truly dreadful sight. After I recovered from the shock, I stopped and built some shelter and found some food. Suddenly, a tiger jumped out and pounced on top of me. I battled with it till it gave up. I went out in glory and pride. After that I knew I could survive in the jungle. I set off and was teleported home.

Jason Thuku (9)
Burnt Oak Primary School, Gillingham

The Hunt

Once there was a little boy called Arthur and under his pillow he had a magic hole that travelled back in time. 'Off we go! Today we are going into the Stone Age! Wow! That is so cool. We are going to hunt today. Well let's do it!'
He set off on his journey. First he made a stone knife, then he killed a mammoth and made some clothes. Next he made a fire and some wood camps and they were fun. It was nearly time to go so he went through the hole, downstairs and told Mum.

Arthur Patey (7)
Burnt Oak Primary School, Gillingham

Cereal Comes Alive

One morning, I heard a banging noise then I wandered downstairs. It was tragic! A piece of Krave! It was alive. I couldn't believe what I was seeing. After that, the Krave attacked me. Then I got bitten by a chicken. I turned around and it was the cornflakes chicken. 'It's too much now!' I shouted.
The cornflakes and Krave stopped. Then the Shreddies lady came in the room and said calmly, 'Just knitting my Shreddies.' Everyone turned to the Shreddies Lady and laughed their heads off. No one stopped laughing for the rest of the week!

Louis Stuart Mills (9)
Burnt Oak Primary School, Gillingham

The Stonehenge

There was once a mum and dad with two little children and they really wanted to see Stonehenge. It took an hour to get there, it took a really long time. When they got there they were a bit scared but still carried on. They saw that it was a massive, beautiful, lovely and good place. They loved it but then they had to go home. It was very tiring. They had to walk for an hour again. When they got back they had something to eat and a drink and then they all went to bed.

Lauren Groot (8)
Burnt Oak Primary School, Gillingham

The Stone Age Brothers

Once upon a time there were two Stone Age brothers and they knew nothing about humans. One of them suddenly saw a human.

'What are you?' said Jeff and Bob.

'I'm human,' said the human. 'Come and meet my friend,' said the human and they went to a dinosaur.

'That is our friend,' said the brothers. 'Anyway it was nice meeting you or should I say very nice.' The Stone Age brothers went home.

'That was very strange,' said Jeff, and they had a good life and lived happily ever after.

Adam Hewing-Everitt (8)
Burnt Oak Primary School, Gillingham

The Last Brick For Stonehenge!

In my house I played with rocks and said, 'Jeff, you have made Stonehenge.' My family didn't help with Stonehenge because they didn't want to.

One day, when I was old enough, I was asked to carry the last block for Stonehenge. I was so happy! I held the block with more men. The townspeople were looking. We travelled from grass fields and we felt like we were going to die. At last we made it, we lifted the rock. We then went back to town and cheered, 'Hooray! Hooray! Well done everyone who helped!'

Ethan Gosney (8)
Burnt Oak Primary School, Gillingham

Dinosaur!

Dinosaurs stomp, chomp and roar but one day a girl came and she didn't see any dinosaurs. When she saw a T-rex coming her way she shouted, 'Help me, please. Help, I'm scared. Get me out of here now!'...

'I'm home at last,' she said. 'Now I can never go on an adventure again because it is very scary when I go on adventures. They are really scary. I like school better than dinosaur adventures. I will go to school tomorrow instead of going on an adventure - school is much better!'

Ella Chelsea Szalajko (8)
Burnt Oak Primary School, Gillingham

The Last Rock Is Placed

One sunny day, everyone got up really early so they could get the rock on before noon. We were in tents because it was easier to get to Stonehenge. It was lunch when we got the last rock on. After lunch, Mum, Dad, Sister and Brother were setting up the party. I wasn't allowed to because I was too small, even though I was five. I was pleased with my hair whilst my parents and sister and brother set up the party.

It was seven o'clock, that meant the party was starting. Soon it was time for bed.

Isabelle Rose Ongley (8)
Burnt Oak Primary School, Gillingham

Kind Kings And Queens

Once there were two special people. One was called Cuby and the other one was called Riley. They were king and queen. They were kind, they let people come to eat and drink. They looked at the view, they were really high. One day some naughty people came who liked fighting kings and queens. The king and queen hammered all the wood they could find so the men got fed up and ran away. The king and queen took all the wood off and the nails. They ate a roast for their dinner and let more people come for breakfast.

Ellie Beth Hales-Ward (8)
Burnt Oak Primary School, Gillingham

Home Finding

First, Arthur, Elizabeth and Peter walked safely to Scotland in Skara Brae. They passed through fields. Finally, Elizabeth, Peter and Arthur started hunting the houses. Peter was scared to get killed by it collapsing on him. They loved hunting but didn't like the food. Elizabeth liked all animals like reptiles, mammals and fish. Arthur was different, he was fun and talented. He didn't like having light spaces. They had to go to sleep because it was 9.30pm. Elizabeth was telling stories.

Charlotte Elizabeth Tucker (7)
Burnt Oak Primary School, Gillingham

The Discovery Of The Skull Head Dragon

One day, I strolled to the sunny beach. I discovered a skull dragon head which gave me one wish. I wished I could have super powers to save the day. I heard screaming coming from the city so I went to see what was happening at the city. I flew to the city to save the day. When I got there I saw an alien destroying the city. I used my laser eyes to save the day and flew him back to space. Then someone came to me and said, 'Can I be your sidekick?'
I said, 'Yes.'

Bnyad Hawkar Salar (9)
Burnt Oak Primary School, Gillingham

The Last Stone Of Stonehenge

It was a sunny day and I was looking at Stonehenge. My mum asked me to put the last stone on Stonehenge. I was super excited to hear that but as soon as I was going to put it on, a very big storm came. I was very angry because I really wanted Stonehenge to be finished. Luckily, the storm came and went very quickly. When I had put it on, my family all stood there looking at Stonehenge. We were very proud of it. People from far and wide came to Stonehenge. I think everyone enjoyed it.

Cassie Owen (8)
Burnt Oak Primary School, Gillingham

The Jungle

One day, I woke up to find myself in a jungle. Surprisingly it was silent. Then I discovered a magical ladybird and it could speak. I scooped it into my hand and asked her if she could show me around. She introduced me to her family, then her friend Ant and her other friend, a lion. I asked, 'Won't he eat you?'
She replied, 'No of course not!'
I made friends with all of the animals and they all liked me. I fell asleep and woke up in my own protective house again with my own family.

Jessica Rhianne Poole (9)
Burnt Oak Primary School, Gillingham

The Lost Treasure

One day there was a pirate, he was fishing and he caught a map. It said that there was treasure so he followed where it went. It went to the death island so he ran away from skeletons and the bad people. It was not easy. He ran away from lots of sharks, but he saw a megalodon shark and he nearly got eaten. He saw the treasure and ran back home.

Domas Urbonas
Burnt Oak Primary School, Gillingham

A Weird Day

I woke up and noticed a tiger in my room from my cereal box. It ran round and started to talk. He said, 'My name is Stripy.' He started to run. I followed him until he went to a jungle called Tiland. I saw parrots, his friends, and many more. Then Stripy called out my name. It was Lily! So I jumped on his back and ran home.

Millie Herve (8)
Burnt Oak Primary School, Gillingham

Space

I was ready to blast off, I stared at the moon. I headed to space, this was my life's dream. I felt so excited I nearly burst out in tears. I landed on the moon with just enough power to get home. On the moon I saw lime-green aliens, also a three-eyed illuminated monster, he ran towards me like a mad bull. I leapt back into the rocket and landed in the seat. I took off and found myself in a meteor shower. I dodged all the meteors but nearly got hit, but I landed safely.

Hannah Rebecca-May Joseph (9)
Burnt Oak Primary School, Gillingham

The Horrific Witch

I woke up and found myself in a yellow bag with loads of people screaming loudly in the bag. I found a sharp, shiny knife and ripped the bag open for the children and me to get out. I ran away from the horrible witch that was going to eat us for her dinner. We sneakily went away from the wicked witch. Then she saw us and she ran, and we ran as fast as we could to our little hut. We had our own dinner and then we killed her, and that was the end.

Ruby Skillings (8)
Burnt Oak Primary School, Gillingham

Ancient Egyptians

Today I was roaming around and I caught my eye on an awesome pyramid full of sand blocks, and you should see the sky! It was as blue as a sapphire. I saw a golden pharaoh staring at me and I was freaked out. I was so scared! After that I was eating fish and bread and I saw loads of mummies wrapped up. I saw the Sphinx, Tutankhamun, hieroglyphics and even the Valley of the Kings! I also witnessed a mummification, it was so cool but a bit gruesome. There was a lot of blood dripping.

David Gracio (10)
Burnt Oak Primary School, Gillingham

The Nasty Witch

I woke up to a loud, deafening scream. I looked out the window and I saw a witch. I got scared. I ran down the stairs and the bag was moving. I pulled out a pocket knife and I tore it open. Suddenly, all my friends jumped out the bag and I said, 'Run for your lives!' Happily I saved all of my friends. Then I realised the witch had horse hooves and I laughed. I really felt proud of myself. I had a bit of fun and chopped off the witch's legs.

Lauren Springham (9)
Burnt Oak Primary School, Gillingham

Come On

'Come on everyone. We are going on a school trip!' I shouted. It would be awesome.
We all got our coats and bags and went. When we were in twos we all went downstairs in silence. All of us stepped into the time traveller - *poof!*
'Wow!' everyone said.
Everyone got to talk. I made a friend named Mary. We all saw the last stone put down in Stonehenge. We put down stones and watched the sunrise, it was beautiful. I was sad to say goodbye to Mary but I managed. Stonehenge will be with me forever.

Grace Oliver (7)
Burnt Oak Primary School, Gillingham

My Dragon Adventure

I realised I was at the beach with my greyhound Frank. I found a dragon skull, and I had an idea. I pulled the dragon's tooth and the mouth opened with a portal inside. When I got inside I was in a cave full of dragons. I sneaked past one of the dragons but there were a hundred more. All of a sudden, they woke up and I screamed so loud like a monster. Surprisingly they flew away, looking very silly and terrified. I then strode back to my house, watched TV then did my homework.

Louie Allen-Fox (9)
Burnt Oak Primary School, Gillingham

The Friendly

One lovely day there was a little girl. She was the princess of the sea. Her dad was the king of the sea and he was very protective, he wouldn't let his daughter, Ella, go up to land at all. However Ella's dad wondered what Ella did when he was not looking. He asked his friend Sam to play with her and follow her.
The next day, Sam saw Ella. She went to a shipwreck looking for jewels like pearls. Later that day, she went home and her dad was happy that she was home.

Izzie Baker (8)
Burnt Oak Primary School, Gillingham

The Dinosaurs

One day I woke up, I saw dinosaurs everywhere. I went out and saw millions of dinosaurs running everywhere. At the back of everything was a T-rex. He was huge so I hid in my house. He ran past me so I went hunting for him. I ran one way but it spotted me. It ran after me. The dinosaurs stopped and ran into the trees and jumped up in the trees. The T-rex spotted every dinosaur. The tree was massive, then an explosion happened. It was the end of the dinosaurs and everything died.

Jakub Henry Darmovzal-Chadwick (8)
Burnt Oak Primary School, Gillingham

The Victorian Princess

Once there was a Victorian princess. She looked out of her window and her family was outside waiting for her. The princess was shocked because her garden was covered in beautiful decorations. She ran outside into her enormous garden to her family. All of a sudden, a carriage turned up with her family from Scotland in it. The only problem was that her family from Scotland didn't recognise her because they hadn't seen the princess and her family for so long. She then showed them pictures of her when she was little. They then magically remembered who she was.

Frankie Jane Pearl Douglas (8)
Burnt Oak Primary School, Gillingham

A Long, Long Time Ago

Once there lived 101 dinosaurs, they were all friends. Elizabeth, she was lost, no one could find her but a few months later this strange person called Bob found her and cooked her for dinner. Bob called it Dino Dinner. Bob thought it was extremely nice and soon there were only 100 dinosaurs left! They were so sad, Elizabeth died because she was the best dinosaur ever. After she died they had a dinosaur festival and there was a song called 'Baby We've Got Bad Luck'. They put it on because Elizabeth liked that song, it was her favourite.

Saffron Tyrone (8)
Burnt Oak Primary School, Gillingham

Florence Nightingale

Once there was a little girl called Florence, she was the most beautiful lady. She wanted to be a great nurse and she was determined to be a nurse. When she was in Year 5 and was learning about nurses and people that were sick, she learned quick and she had great handwriting.
When she was a teenage girl, she said she was going to get a job. Her friends knew she was going to be a great and awesome nurse because she was a great cleaner and a good girl.

Samira Mariam Jah (8)
Burnt Oak Primary School, Gillingham

Untitled

One day I woke up to find myself in a boat. Suddenly, I heard a crash. The boat was filling up with water. Then I remembered I had one wish. I wished that the boat would stop filling up with water. *Bang!* It stopped and started sinking. As I looked out the window, there were sharks... I screamed, 'Save me!'
In a flash, a superhero came and saved me. I felt lucky.
The next day, I woke up and I was at my home. I said, 'Home sweet home.' I was so relieved. Now I can sleep, finally...

Sophie Woollett (9)
Burnt Oak Primary School, Gillingham

World War One

The train station was empty. No one was around, therefore it was soundless. I stood quietly waiting for the dusty train to arrive. After a while, I decided to quickly go outside to look for help, however nobody was there. Suddenly, a derelict house caught fire. Consequently, I anxiously sprinted back to the train station. As I was running back I saw a car in the distance, at first I thought that I was just imagining things but I wasn't. Eventually, the car had stopped right by me. There was a man, he took me to a nice family.

Lillie-Rose Manley (11)
Burnt Oak Primary School, Gillingham

Back In Time!

Yesterday I woke up and realised I was in a boat. It was the amazing Titanic. It was a minute away from sinking! The alarms went crazy. I ran to a lifeboat and I jumped quickly in. 'Argh!' I screamed loudly. I was petrified.

Then, all of a sudden, Captain Dillan came but at the same time evil Mr Porkchop came. They had a Titanic battle.

A few minutes later, Mr Porkchop died. Then Captain Dillan came to help us. He carried us to our houses. Hooray for Captain Dillan.

Dillan Hedges (8)
Burnt Oak Primary School, Gillingham

Queen Elizabeth II

In a castle far away, in a massive field full of trees and flowers, lived a beautiful queen who was loved by loads of people in the village on the edge of the field. She was despised by one person, however, that was Chockle. He hated every queen in the world and nobody knew why, except the rest of his gang. He hadn't told anyone else. He made a mission to kill Queen Elizabeth II at a football game.

It was the day of the game and... it didn't work.

Shannan Lee Bridget Batson (10)
Burnt Oak Primary School, Gillingham

One Wish

Yesterday I was strolling along the sandy beach, then suddenly I discovered a mythical dragon skull. I thought I was dreaming because I was granted a wish. I didn't have that much money, so I wished for endless amounts of money. Later that day, everywhere I went there was money. I thought that was too much so I spent it every day, until I spent it all. I went back to the dragon and explained to him that I wanted no more money, so he took all of the money and I never went to the beach ever again.

Ellie Jefford (9)
Burnt Oak Primary School, Gillingham

Stone Age Child

Jack and his friends and family were getting ready to put the last stone down but when they put it down it fell down on them. Because they were so strong they lifted it up again. Then Jack rammed it into the hole and they pushed the rock into the hole so it would stand up properly. They were so happy that they burst out with so much laughter. Then they lay down and went to sleep and they actually went to sleep, and they lived happily ever after.

Michaela Mardel (8)
Burnt Oak Primary School, Gillingham

Stonehenge

In my little house I was playing with my rocks. My mum and my brother always went to help build Stonehenge and I always wanted to go and help, but I was too young.

One day I was able to go and it was the final piece! We walked in the sun and ran in the rain. We dashed through the cold and finally we made it. The wind was so cold that it was very hard to put it in. After that, we travelled for hours back home and we will always remember that special day.

Patryk Bielski (9)
Burnt Oak Primary School, Gillingham

The Golden Pyramid

'This is magnificent, but what is that?' I said, glancing around the tomb at the fantastic drawings as the light bounced off the treasures.

'I have no idea,' my best mate replied.

Quietly but casually, we walked towards what seemed like a golden chest.

'Dear me, Sir, aren't you afraid of what could be in there?' my mate asked.

'Why no. As long as it is historic, I have no problem,' I replied.

We lifted the cover off the chest.

'This is a body, Sir,' he exclaimed.

'My friend, we have discovered the body of a king! Pharaoh Tutankhamun.'

Jasmine Thuku (11)
Burnt Oak Primary School, Gillingham

Untitled

In the time of the cavemen, where there were no trees to be seen, lived a caveman called Yaashwant. He went out to search for food. He soon had supper and he began walking home. He came across a vicious beast of the jungle, a tiger, and ran into a big tree. He climbed it so the tiger couldn't get him. He then thought if he tamed it he could survive every constant attack by animals. He took a bone and threw it to the tiger. The tiger chewed it and he was never worried again...

Yaashwant Selvaradjou (9)
Burnt Oak Primary School, Gillingham

Untitled

Bang! Boom! Planes flying and dropping bombs, guns firing, people dropping dead. The Blitz had started! 'Wipe them out!' demanded the general.
It all started when the English bombed the German boats. Now they wanted revenge.
'There's too many of them,' yelled General Johnson.
'Prepare for battle,' shouted the pilot.
Machine guns shot my wings. 'I've lost control. I'm going down, mayday, I'm going down!' I yelled to the radio. I pulled my parachute and survived.
Days passed, the war had finished. We won. They surrendered, they were scared. Apparently their leader committed suicide. They rescued me. I needed help.

Kieran Waters (10)
Burnt Oak Primary School, Gillingham

The Past Is Mad!

Once upon a time Lillie went to a scientist to make a time machine. Lillie was a princess so she got what she wanted. A week later she came to see it. Mr Mad, the scientist said, 'Here.'

She slipped through the portal. She was in ancient Egypt! She met a young boy, his name was Pino.

'Hi,' screamed Pino.

They went to a pyramid. 'A code,' they screamed.

'I know what it means.'

Bing-bong!

'OK, let's go.'

Boom!

'Now we're in China!'

They danced then Lillie heard the queen and king crying so they went home.

Lillie Spinks (7)
Burnt Oak Primary School, Gillingham

Ancient Egypt

One sunny, warm day, a camel and his family were roaming around the desert. The sand was scorching-hot but the camels were used to it.

However, one camel wasn't very happy. He wasn't very happy about his life. His family, who thought that the camel was great with what he had got in his life, tried to encourage the camel to feel better about himself but nothing actually worked. Sadly, the upset camel walked off.

Rapidly, he sprinted towards the Nile. He saw his reflection and felt much better because he knew his life was great.

Melissa Woolley (10)
Burnt Oak Primary School, Gillingham

The End Of Cleopatra

'Let's begin the mummification,' announced Cleopatra.

The helpful guards began to mummify the dead body. They stuck a hook up the recently deceased person's nose. After that, they hooked the brain and out it came. A few minutes later the mummification had finished.

Half an hour later, Cleopatra strolled out of the temple and gazed around curiously looking for a snake. Once she had found the poisonous monster, she whispered, 'It's time to leave, time to let someone else be pharaoh.'

A few seconds later, the dagger-toothed snake bit Cleopatra, therefore she was dead.

Courtney Hook (11)
Burnt Oak Primary School, Gillingham

The Adventure

One morning, Heather was reading her Victorian book, it was about the Victorian times. It was lunch for Heather and she went to a restaurant. For pudding, she had raspberry ripple ice cream. Afterwards, she went home and read her book. Suddenly a storm came out of her book, it washed her inside the book. The storm finished and Heather stared at the people, they were dressed weirdly and she realised she was in her book. A lady said, 'What's wrong?'
Heather answered the lady and the lady used her magic to help Heather get back. It was an adventure.

Kelly Xu (8)
Burnt Oak Primary School, Gillingham

She's Gone Now

Cleopatra walked outside and cautiously looked around. Suddenly... a bite. A large venomous snake was digging his daggers into her feet. Cleopatra screamed and fell to the floor in pain. Her whole foot turned purple. She could no longer feel any pain in her foot but it was crawling up her leg. Her scream turned into only a whisper. The pain, almost at her head. Then, her head lifted up; the look of nausea on her face. Her head dropped. The shadow of death had fallen upon her. Silence. She was out of time...

Abigail Westcott (10)
Burnt Oak Primary School, Gillingham

Strong Vs Strong

The carpenter said the French were going to attack so they should get ready to fight. Julius Caesar got ready to fight. They got their strongest fighters but they were injured so he went to find some more. He could not find anyone. He kidnapped some from Holland, Russia and France but it was hard. Then France attacked. It was a fierce and bloody fight. They both used 100 fighters and 50 horses. Italy was falling behind because they had now got 20 and then Caesar came and killed everyone, including their king.

Paul Manu (9)
East Stour Primary School, Ashford

The Story Of Osiris' Death

Osiris and Isis loved their country of Ancient Egypt dearly, but Osiris' brother Seth was always in the shadow of his sibling. Seth wanted to be king, he started to hatch a cunning plan. Grinning, Seth told his friends if they helped him they would be rich. He organised a grand feast. Seth asked everyone to try and fit in a bewitching, beautiful box. Nobody fitted apart from Osiris, and when no one was looking, Seth slammed the lid down then claimed it for himself.
When night fell, Seth carried the box and threw it in the Nile. Osiris died.

Frankie Jada Griffiths (9)
East Stour Primary School, Ashford

King Henry VIII

King Henry VIII was a young man when he became king. He loved sports, he was very slim and he enjoyed feasting. But what he really wanted was a son. Henry had six wives, his first wife's name was Catherine and she had one daughter called Mary. Next Henry married Anne, she also had a girl called Elizabeth. Unfortunately, Anne got her head chopped off. The third wife had a boy called Edward but the last three didn't have babies. After years of eating food, Henry got ill and died and the last wife survived.

Jack George (8)
East Stour Primary School, Ashford

King Tut's Sudden Death

One day, Akenaten died and Tutankhamun was pharaoh and he was only nine or ten years old. He restored all the gods that his father banned. He became the most popular pharaoh ever but somehow he suddenly died. Everyone rushed to create his tomb. When everything was finished in time, the tomb was sealed but no one knew how he'd died. They were determined to find out though so everyone rushed to see if they could find out how he died. Did they find out...?

Samantha Knapman (8)
East Stour Primary School, Ashford

The Egyptian Grave Robber

Once there was a very skilful grave robber. His identity was unknown and he had robbed many graves. Whenever he needed something he could always afford it. He only had to rob Tutankhamun's tomb and then he would have robbed everything. The next day, he went to the pharaoh's tomb and opened the coffin, but was caught by a slave and the tomb was saved. After that, the robber was arrested. Then he was thrown in the River Nile and drowned.

Joseph Barrett (9)
East Stour Primary School, Ashford

Osiris And Isis In Ancient Egypt

In ancient Egypt, Osiris and Isis lived in a town of joy but Osris's brother Seth always brought evil to their town. He just wanted to be ruler of Osiris and Isis's town. Seth told Osiris's villagers they would be rich if they would help him with this evil plot. Seth put together a feast. Everyone was invited. Osiris and Isis were enjoying their party and Seth had a game of: 'Who can fit in the shiny, golden box'. Seth made it perfectly Osiris's size. He was the only one that could fit in the box. Did the plan work...?

Lois-Grace Knight (9)
East Stour Primary School, Ashford

The Giant Surprise

Long ago, in ancient Egypt, a pharaoh called Osiris had a wife called Isis. One day, Osiris went to find food then got attacked by a cheetah and died.
Isis on the other hand was worried. She searched for him but couldn't find him. One day, while she was lying peacefully in the woodland breeze, Osiris came out of the bush and said, 'Sorry I tricked you. I didn't mean to scare you but I've been here for ten years. Let's go home now.'

Louise April Gadd (8)
East Stour Primary School, Ashford

Germans Defeated

In 1942, Charlie and the other soldiers were getting ready for war. Suddenly, he saw some strange people in the distance. Charlie saw Hitler's sign! Luckily he wasn't seen. When they got to the battlefield, Charlie made a plan. He got together his friends and borrowed some artefacts from a museum. He went in a plane and used the artefacts as puppets. Then Hitler and his soldiers ran to their boats and sailed away.

Holly Apps (8)
East Stour Primary School, Ashford

The Sun God Ra

There once was a sun god called Ra. If people worshipped him and were scared of him he was happy to let them live their lives. But people stopped worshipping him and they stopped being scared of him, so Ra sent his daughter Hathor to eat them. Hathor appeared in the form of a huge heart-tearing lioness. She killed everyone that stopped worshipping Ra but she developed a thirst for human blood. Ra had to act fast. He filled the Nile with wine and Hathor saw it and went home. Egypt was spared. Today the Nile sometimes floods wine.

Jake Freeman (9)
East Stour Primary School, Ashford

The Gods Of Egypt

In ancient Egypt, Osiris and Isis loved their country, but Osiris's brother Seth was jealous of him because he wanted to be king. Full of pure darkness, Seth told his friends to help him and they would get rich. He organised a feast, it was a plot. He asked everyone to try and fit into the golden box, but no one could fit in there. When Osiris tried getting in, he fitted. Suddenly, Seth slammed the lid shut!
When the night fell, Seth carried the box to the Nile, he threw it in! Seth then became king.

Tommy Randall (8)
East Stour Primary School, Ashford

The Ancient Egyptian King

The ancient Egyptians once had a king called Tutankhamun. He had a father and a mother who died so there was no one to look after him. He died unexpectedly at the age of nineteen. The tomb had to be made quickly. The tomb was made in such a rush that the paintings didn't even have time to dry! When the tomb was finished, there were black marks all over the tomb.

Orlando Caka (9)
East Stour Primary School, Ashford

World War One Disaster!

In France, a girl called Jodie was nineteen and a boy called John was nineteen as well. Germany and England were going to war and John went; he was one of the people.
Afterwards, some very sad news came in a postcard to say John had died. He died not knowing he had two children called Finnlay and Frankie. They were both two years old and did not understand their mother's news. They understood when they were five because they saw a picture of their heroic dad.

Macy Patterson (9)
East Stour Primary School, Ashford

Tiny Tim Sees Adam And Eve

One day there lived a boy called Tiny Tim. He saw a doll's house then he pressed a button but this wasn't any doll's house, it had powers. A few minutes later, he opened his eyes and saw gardens and in the gardens there were two people named Adam and Eve. They were eating fruit. Suddenly Tim saw a bright light in the sky, it was God. They were getting told off because he didn't want them to eat the fruit. They disobeyed God and they got out of the garden because they weren't able to live there.

Darcey Taylor-Kirk (9)
East Stour Primary School, Ashford

The Big Heroes

It was a very cold day. It was so hard to fight. Harry and Millie were fighting in World War One. They got a bit tired of fighting so asked their parents if they could give up fighting. They just got mad.
One day there was a bigger war, it was the huge 'War of the Bear'. There were guns and bows and arrows. Harry got hurt. He was in hospital the next day. Millie missed Harry so Millie went to see Harry and gave him a kiss. They then gave up fighting for the rest of their lives.

Keira Harman (8)
East Stour Primary School, Ashford

The Sandy Desert

'The sandy desert,' I gasped, staring across the water to the shiny beach glistening in the distance.
'What do you think, Boss?' my first friend said to me.
'It's so beautiful,' I replied. 'A world where we can build a new city that will know God's laws and follow them. Here we can be safe.'
'Aren't you scared, Boss?'
'What of?' I replied.
'The Vikings,' said my friend. 'Most people say they are savages.'
'Then we will teach them everything we know. They'll be part of our sandy desert as well, as long as they follow our rules.'

Ellie Shaw (9)
East Stour Primary School, Ashford

The Ending Of World War One!

It was nearly over, suddenly the Germans attacked and there were screams of horror. A lot of people died and two soldiers were left. They hid in the trench half-flooded already. One was a German and he was shot. The Englishman helped him up. He thought it was all over.
'Thanks for that and the food,' he said, struggling to talk.
The Englishman cried, 'It's OK.'
They ran away.
'I'm so glad it's over and I get to see my wife Shara.'

Chloe Louise Hughes (8)
East Stour Primary School, Ashford

Beowulf's Last Battle!

In Denmark we were getting attacked, then I met the courageous hero Beowulf. We had to fight for our country. It was amazing fighting alongside Beowulf. The fight against Grendel was hard. I made it through, unfortunately Beowulf died and it was my turn to shine in the spotlight. I knew it would be hard to fight alone...

Isobel Boorman (9)
East Stour Primary School, Ashford

World War One Fight

In World War One, soldiers went to different countries to fight. In England, a man went away to France to fight against them. The man was called Darpan and he missed his girlfriend, Keira. Darpan sent a postcard to Keira, it said, 'I miss you very much. I hope I came back soon.' Keira was doing the washing up when the postcard came through the post.
Finally, at Christmas, the fighting stopped. Darpan went home to see Keira at Keira's house and when he arrived, Keira came to the door and they kissed. Darpan then went back to war.

Millie Smith (9)
East Stour Primary School, Ashford

Dinosaurs And The Gigantic Meteor

Once upon a time dinosaurs ruled the Earth, then suddenly a disaster came. A meteor crashed into Earth and the dinos died out. Only two survived, they battled to the death but as they were fighting they both realised something that was important, really important. They could become really good friends. Firstly they thought they could not become friends, then they actually became the best of best friends!

Shaun Ellesmere (8)
East Stour Primary School, Ashford

The Death Of Osiris

Osiris and Isis loved their country and cared for it with all their hearts. However, Osiris's brother, Seth, was full of pure jealousy and darkness. He told his friends that if they helped him they'd be rich so they agreed. One day, Seth threw a party and anyone who fit in the chest won. But only Osiris fitted. Then Seth slammed the lid shut as if he won, then threw the coffin away and Osiris died. But Isis was determined to find out what really happened to her husband.

Alex Ojo (8)
East Stour Primary School, Ashford

George The Fierce Knight

Once upon a time there was a boy called George who was a fierce knight. One foggy morning, George set off through the forest and a fire-breathing dragon crept behind him. This was the biggest dragon he had ever seen. The dragon pounced up in front of him and pulled his leg and tried to eat it. George tried to pull his leg away but the dragon was too strong for George...

Freddie Masters (8)
East Stour Primary School, Ashford

The Ruling Of Osiris And Isis

In ancient Egypt, Osiris and Isis ruled. Their town was full of joy! Osiris's brother, Seth, was so jealous that one day he told some of his friends if they would help him they would be rich. This cunning plot was no rubbish plot, it was evil!
One day, Seth arranged a party at the palace. That day the hall of the palace was so beautifully decorated. Soon, at the party, some men walked in with a large box and asked everyone to try and fit inside. None of them fitted. Osiris tried and he was perfect. Then...

Rebecca Chapple (8)
East Stour Primary School, Ashford

The Egyptian Adventure

One dark, gloomy night in Egypt, in a magnificent pyramid, there was a girl named Jessica who loved exploring and wanted to go and see Tutankhamun. The night she snuck into the tomb and she was amazed, so she sneakily took some treasure! As she walked back out the tomb, she wondered if the mummy would come to her... After that she put the treasure on her shelf and fell asleep...

Jessica Griffiths (9)
East Stour Primary School, Ashford

Untitled

Once there was a caveman called Takarr and he hunted a mammoth. He almost got killed by the blood-hungry sabre-toothed tiger. After that, he rode a mammoth around the cold bits of Canada. He met some people in the land Oros. Their names were Sasha, Tensay, Jaymar, Urki and Karoosh.
One day, Jaymar the hunter got a disease from an animal she'd hunted earlier in the day. She was feeling ill and she couldn't hunt food for herself so she asked Takarr to get food for her because she was very, very ill.

Kyle Endicott (9)
East Stour Primary School, Ashford

The Time Travelling Girl

One night, Molly fell asleep and in the morning she woke up in ancient Egypt. A pharaoh was calling, 'Molly, Molly, go and build my pyramid!'
Molly went outside and built a tomb just like one she had seen in her Egyptian book. Sadly, the pharaoh didn't like it and chased her with a sword. She hid behind a huge sarcophagus and the pharaoh ran straight past her. She curled up and went to sleep in the corner.
When she woke again, she felt her soft bunny toy under her arm and was back in her own bed.

Ella Darlington (9)
East Stour Primary School, Ashford

Going To The Foundling Hospital!

It's Monday, I wake up and jump onto Jim because I love him. We jump onto Mum and Dad who are sad because we are going shopping.
'No Mum, don't say all of us are going to stay at the Foundling Hospital and we're coming back in seven years time!'
After we are off the belly-churning train, we enter the Foundling Hospital.
After seven years, mine and Jim's family are let out of the Foundling Hospital to go and live back with Mother and Father in the big and empty farmhouse.

Nandika Thileepan (9)
East Stour Primary School, Ashford

The Soldier Who Found The Mysterious Castle

Once a soldier called Beowulf lived in a little house in the middle of a forest. One day he decided to go on an adventure and found a castle made from stone. He went in and had a look around, and found a soldier called Rex. They had a fight, but when the fight stopped they became friends. They fought the king and won the battle. They had the castle all to themselves. They lived happily in the lovely garden full of flowers, bees and butterflies. In the end, they all got their own share of money, gold and silver.

Casey Marlow (9)
East Stour Primary School, Ashford

The Tomb Of Doom...

In the night two robbers crept into a pyramid, their names were Ruby and Pearls. They were trying to rob the tomb of King Kufufull! To get in, they dug a hole in the sand, which led to the tomb's floor. But after some walking, Ruby set off a trap which made the floor move to reveal lava! To escape, they swung across a rope to get to safety. When they looked up they saw the door, after they opened it they went inside and robbed. They happily then got out and ran away with the treasure to their home.

Beatrice McCarthy (9)
East Stour Primary School, Ashford

The Silly Explorer Jim

A silly explorer called Jim always tried his best, but sadly things never went right for him. He thought he had found a bone but when he showed it to other people they giggled because it was obviously a fake. So Jim ran into the jungle and said, 'I'm so dumb!'
'No you're not,' said a voice from above. 'I'll help you become a real explorer. I know where some real bones are.'
Jim found a huge real bone and took it back to the exhibition. He became a world-famous bone collector.

Kelsie-Jae Hodges (9)
East Stour Primary School, Ashford

The Maid Who Tried To Escape

Millie was peacefully cleaning up as usual. Suddenly, her master and mistress came in furiously. They accused her of stealing. 'I honestly have not done anything!' exclaimed Millie.
However they ignored her. They decided that she should be burnt in an enormously giant fire.
In a dash she ran away. Millie, who was quite terrified, thought she had found an extremely brilliant hiding place. When all of a sudden a fierce guard spotted her, so he charged straight towards her. She knew, however, he was quite slow. Because of that, she thought she could escape but could she really...?

Samina Thebe (9)
East Stour Primary School, Ashford

Romans In Britain

One morning Gabriel was searching for food in the dark and dusty forest. He heard a squeak and the bush moved. A small pig jumped out of it. He was cute and Gabriel named him Max. Suddenly, he saw some Roman soldiers passing by so he hid in a big hollowed trunk with Max. He took Max home and knocked on the door, but was worried because he didn't have any food. His mum screamed at him and she sent him back out. He went to a farmer and asked for food. The farmer gave him some food.

Rayan Aziz (9)
East Stour Primary School, Ashford

The Slave

Lizzy was sweeping slowly like a snail. She was sold as a slave when she was just two years old. A woman adopted her.
Lizzy's thoughts were that the woman would take care of her nicely. The woman's name was Lia. She did take care of her until Lia became queen. Lia treated Lizzy like a slave again. She met other slaves named Varda, Osiris and Timmy. Lizzy thought that she heard Osiris before. But he said, 'Don't worry about that!'
A few years later, Lia died so it was the king's choice to pick one of the girl slaves.

Nuyem Chemjong (9)
East Stour Primary School, Ashford

Are Marlo's Parents Slaves Or Saved?

Marlo woke up to screaming. He looked out of his window and saw his parents tied to a tree. As quick as a flash he got dressed and ran downstairs and out the door. He hid behind a tree and saw his parents being taken onto a ship. He ran as fast as he could and, just in time, he got on board and took the rope, and tied it in the ground using an African knot. Then he untied his parents and they all ran back to their house and double locked the door.

Anevay Gravesande-Whyte (8)
East Stour Primary School, Ashford

House Bang

Charlie Five Nine One built a house made of wood. A creeper blew his house up. Charlie went to go on an adventure to find better materials. He fought a skeleton then got some bones. He found a dog. He called the dog Max. Max got some more materials for Charlie. They went back and made a brand-new house made of wood and some cobblestones. They started from the top and made their way down. They added the door in. They put the floor down with red carpet and decorated the lovely house. Charlie was very happy.

Jack Norfolk (10)
The Gordon Schools Federation, Rochester

The Demon Dog

I tiptoed up to the attic where the wailing sounds were coming from. The door opened and a picture came into view. It was a picture of a street full of ghosts. I reached out to touch the smooth surface but my hand slipped through. I stepped out onto a dusty road. I looked up and saw a sign saying the year: '2116'. I was exactly 1000 years into the future. Suddenly, a person floated through me. They were all ghosts! I walked onwards. A black shape came prowling towards me. It was the Demon Dog coming to get me...

Ella Wills (10)
The Gordon Schools Federation, Rochester

The Easter Party

'Wake up!' shouted Simon. It was time for camp so they got up and dressed. Suddenly, they heard shouting so they walked outside. It was the coach shouting at Thedor, the coach of the party. The chocolate had gone missing.

Then the coach came over (this can't be good). She said, 'Can you please go on an adventure to find the eggs?'

Off they set on the adventure. They were marching through mud and everything. They finally got to the top of the mountains. There they got all the eggs and it was the best party ever. 'Hooray!'

Ellie Louise Fox (9)
The Gordon Schools Federation, Rochester

The Mystery Of The Lost Eggs

'Wake up, it's Easter!' shouted Thomas and Kyle, as they got up. 'Let's find the Easter eggs.' They looked around the whole house, in the garden and at their nan's flat, but nothing. Suddenly, they realised it could have been the Easter bunny because the Easter bunny had to give eggs to the other kids. Suddenly, Thomas noticed a sparkle, he ran over and got an egg.

Rubie Harrs (10)
The Gordon Schools Federation, Rochester

The Stadium And Victoria

Oh my gosh! Listen, I went to a Roman stadium... and it was fantastic! Here is the story...

Okay, I was happily sitting in the stadium and a gladiator came on. Oh my bananas! He was so handsome and he was about to fight a strange beast! The beast came on and they were fighting. I felt so sorry, I jumped in, opened the door and told him to poke the beast in his cage. We both closed the door and he won, and now he knows the technique.

Chelsy Victoria Smith (9)
The Gordon Schools Federation, Rochester

The Problem In The Pyramid

Whoosh!

'Uh-oh Joe, a bad storm's coming.'

They start running to find shelter and they come across a marvellous pyramid in the middle of nowhere. 'Come on Joe, let's look around the pyramid.'

'I'll stay here so the door doesn't seem shut.' *Slam!* The door closed with Joe by the door. 'No Joe, why did you let the door close? Now how do we get out? I don't want to die!'

'Let's put our thinking caps on... let's find hard things to hit the door to crack it open.'

'Yes.'

'We're out, let's go home, we're free!'

Jake Mark Lee Thiselton (9)
The Gordon Schools Federation, Rochester

Ancient Romans

In this saga you will find out how a Roman gladiator escapes the big and wrecked Colosseum and how he built an army and lost... It was a cold night at the Colosseum when a Roman came. They opened the wooden door and the gladiator stabbed the guards with a knife and they died. George grabbed the keys and he saw more guards so he took them out and he let the other gladiators out. He raised an army to get revenge on the emperor. He had a good plan but the Romans were stronger and they won!

George Denniss-Baker (9)
The Gordon Schools Federation, Rochester

The Rescue

There was a Roman soldier who lived with his wife. His name was Henry. They both lived in the same house.
A couple of days later, Henry went to war while his wife stayed at home. 'Be safe, Henry!' said his wife, so he went to war.
A few hours later, he was still at war but then the other team of the Romans, who were the enemies, came into the village and captured Henry's wife. Henry came home. He didn't see her. He heard her scream. He found her. 'Henry!' He saved her and kissed her on the lips.

Grace Jagger (8)
The Gordon Schools Federation, Rochester

The Surprise

One special day there lived Daisy, Lulu, Jack, Dad and Mum.
Daisy, Lulu and Jack went to the park. Dad and Mum were
setting up a surprise for Daisy, Lulu and Jack. Mum bought Daisy
and Lulu a phone. Dad bought Jack a PS4. The problem was,
Dad forgot to get the games so Dad went back to get the games.
Dad went back home. Mum got all the things ready. Then Dad
put the games on the PS and Mum put the phones on the table.
Daisy, Lulu and Jack walked in, they were happy.

Daisy-Mae Scott (9)
The Gordon Schools Federation, Rochester

The Discovery

'Oh, yes I will,' screamed Howard Carter, 'I will find the treasure of
Tutankhamun! Yes!'
'Do it then,' sneered the mayor of Cairo.
Howard Carter stormed out of the room.
He trod off into the desert for weeks as he sulked until he came to
a valley. The valley was called the Valley of Kings. 'Ah! The place
where King Tut was buried.' This would be a discovery! He took
out his penknife and headed for the burial place.
He found a hole in the rock. He managed to squeeze through the
hole. He found the chamber and the treasure...

Felix Condy (9)
The Gordon Schools Federation, Rochester

Becoming Friends With Romans

'How are you today?' said Lilly.

'I'm fine,' Hanna replied.

'It's good that all the Romans are gone. We'd better go to sleep.'

Later that night, Hanna and Lilly heard banging outside their house.

'What was that?' said Lilly. They looked out of their window.

The Romans were back! 'I have a plan,' Hanna said, 'come with me.'

They both went to the bakery for a better hiding place. Hanna went up to one of them and said, 'Please stop hurting our people.' He said, 'OK,' and they all became friends and were happy.

Tia Li Riley (9)
The Gordon Schools Federation, Rochester

Leave Us Alone!

'What a lovely day, mates.'

'Do you remember what we have to do today?' shouted Hugo, the leader of the pirates.

'Um yes, Captain,' one of the pirates whispered.

When they arrived, they started stealing food when suddenly... a man, called Jack, went up to the pirates and yelled, 'Why must you invade our country?'

On the other hand, the pirates just laughed. Then Jack said, 'Let's have a sword fight and whoever puts their hands on the floor has to leave.'

Eventually the pirates left Germany forever.

Victoria Ward (8)
The Gordon Schools Federation, Rochester

90

Hade's Victory

There lived a gladiator who didn't like to fight. When he was not fighting he did maths. Hades was nervous, it was his turn to go and fight with Glory. He was a bit frightened. He was strong but not as strong as Glory. To his surprise, he won. Boy oh boy, you had to see his face. The emperor said, 'Hades, you are through to the next round.' Everyone was cheering and Glory was so, so, so angry his face was red. Even the emperor was pleased and said, 'Well done, Hades.'

Amelia Pollard (9)
The Gordon Schools Federation, Rochester

Life In Victorian Times

'I am fed up with this!' shouted Victoria across the room.
'Come on Victoria, it's not that bad,' said her little sister, Elizabeth.
'It is bad!' said Victoria. 'We haven't been to school for almost a year now.'
The door opened, her father Anthony heard shouting.
'What's the matter now?'
'I wish the wars would stop,' said Victoria.
The father laughed, 'Only if you join the army.'
When Victoria called the army, they said she didn't have a chance but they let her. Victoria killed all the enemies. After hours they cheered for her.
'Long live Victoria! Forever! Yay!'

Shakira Bah (8)
The Gordon Schools Federation, Rochester

Caught!

There was a Celtic warrior, named PETE (standing for Petrifying, Enormous, Totally Electrifying) Man. He was one of their top men. He knew how to operate cannons. They were going in for a battle, he took a chance and went to the front of the battlefield but... the Romans had made a sneaky attack. They attacked from the sides. 'Yes! We've got some of them! Now let's get out of here and let the real fighters do the rest.'
'Argh! Let me out of this bag!' said PETE. He escaped then saw it, the Roman gladiator ring. He was victorious!

Joseph Sobanjo (9)
The Gordon Schools Federation, Rochester

The Awakening

'Go, go, go! Get to shelter!' shouted Lee, as everyone hurried past him. *Crash!* Something landed on the roof. I heard screams and gunshots. Adam disappeared as soon as the lights flickered. There was a hole, Lee jumped down it and there was Toxic and Ads.
'Well, well. Nice to see you? Naa!' He held a pistol up to Adam. 'No you wouldn't.' Lee dashed up to Toxic, punched him in the face and grabbed his gun. But then Toxic pointed to the roof, a giant grenade was stuck to it. They escaped. *Boom!*
'Ha ha ha! I'm here!'

Lee Jones (9)
The Gordon Schools Federation, Rochester

War Zone!

Bang!
Something is strange, Paul thought to himself. He found a child and then he ran to him.
'Get in the house, quickly,' he demanded. Paul got in the house just in time, because Hitler was coming! 'I'm Max,' whispered the boy. Paul was confused. Then Max pulled a bomb out of his pocket. 'I will give you this,' called the boy.
Paul took the bomb and saw Hitler. 'I'm going out to get him!' Furiously Paul told Max. He threw the special bomb and Hitler was sucked in.

Ben Penfold (8)
The Gordon Schools Federation, Rochester

Romans Invade

'Ahoy! I can see land!' screamed the Roman captain. 'Are you ready lads?' he shouted once more. 'We shall take the land!'
'But there is a massive wall around it.'
'It's nothing we can't handle anyway, Scotland always comes prepared.'
Without any hesitation, they climbed out and started to fight. Scotland had lots of cannons and the Romans kept getting pushed back. The Romans called for reinforcements but Scotland still won.

Lucca Wade (9)
The Gordon Schools Federation, Rochester

The Caveman!

'Wow, where are we?' asked Lizzie.

'We are in the caveman times!' explained Vicky.

Vicky and Lizzie went to explore. It was too pretty. But... Lizzie saw a huge cake so she ran to retrieve it. She did not realise it was just her imagination! Lizzie suddenly didn't know where she was! She could see someone in the distance.

'Hello?' smiled Lizzie.

'Who are you? Why are you here?' he asked.

'I'm stuck here and I've lost my friend!' she explained.

The caveman helped Lizzie.

After two days... they found Vicky and the girls went home.

Tia Venn (9)
The Gordon Schools Federation, Rochester

Fight Of The Valkyries

General Toop was bored but also excited for his first battle against the mean pirates! As they landed on the beach, a soldier had spotted the pirates. 'Hey look, there over the...' The arrow pierced his heart and he collapsed.

'Battle stations!' the general screamed.

As the battle started, his men were winning but then General Toop was knocked unconscious and taken to the pirates' boss. Toop woke up and found himself on a wooden beheading stand...

Kian Terry (10)
The Gordon Schools Federation, Rochester

Blazing The Fire Dragon

Hi, I'm Evie and I like dragons. One day I found an egg but it wasn't just any old egg, it was a dragon egg, and it had a flame pattern around it. Suddenly, the egg hatched and out came a fire dragon called Blazing.

When Blazing grew up, she took me to the dragon world where all the dragons lived. I had lots of fun. I got to play lots of games with lots of dragons. Soon it was time for bed, so Blazing flew me home to the real world in time for dinner and bed.

Evie Lipscombe (9)
The Gordon Schools Federation, Rochester

A Mummy Awakens

Shaun woke up trapped inside a pyramid. 'What shall I do?' Shaun whispered to himself. Shaun grabbed a torch with a burning-hot flickering flame balancing on the tippy top. An hour later a door appeared and slowly rose open. Shaun travelled down a very long corridor. Suddenly, a foot came around the corner wrapped in bandages; Shaun knew what it was and ran away from the evil and dangerous mummy.

Layla Lola Jones (10)
The Gordon Schools Federation, Rochester

The Dragon Called Kevin

'What are you doing today, Kevin?' said Stuart.
'I'm testing how fast I can go and how much I can control myself.'
'Can I join in?' said Bob.
'I want to race you,' said Dave.
'OK,' said Kevin, 'when I say three. One, two, three...'
'I'm going to beat you,' said Dave.
'Whoever wins gets 20 cookies,' said Kevin.
'20 cookies, I'm definitely going to win,' said Dave.
'No, I am,' said Kevin.
'Just one more to go and I will get through it. I win!' said Kevin.

Ryan Pearton (9)
The Gordon Schools Federation, Rochester

The Tudors

'Catherine of Aragon, I am going to dissolve you as you're not really my kind.' King Henry went to the second lady-in-waiting, her name was Anne Boleyn. She was beheaded as she had a baby girl when Henry wanted a boy.
The next lady-in-waiting was Jane Seymour and Henry loved her the most, as she had a baby boy. Jane died months later.
Anne of Cleves was the next lady. Henry didn't like her.
There was another lady, Catherine Howard, she was beheaded as she had a baby girl. Katherine Parr was Henry's final wife.

Lauren Stevens (10)
The Gordon Schools Federation, Rochester

The Girl Who Met A Dragon!

One beautiful morning there was a girl called Lucy. Lucy's mother asked Lucy to go to the village. Lucy said, 'Mother, haven't you heard the shops have closed?'
'You have to go to the forest to your uncle's.'
Lucy closed the door and went to the forest. It was getting cold and dark and Lucy saw a cave so she went inside. Lucy saw a dragon and the dragon was hungry, so it ate Lucy up.
Lucy's mother heard that her daughter died so she never ever went to the forest again. Lucy's mother missed her.

Roshan Ahmed Shebani (9)
The Gordon Schools Federation, Rochester

The Ancient Pyramid

'Yay! We have reached the perfect space,' said one of the builders, 'this place is called Egypt.'
'Now should we build something here?' asked another builder.
'Yes, we should, so let's start building.'
The builders were getting ready to build the pyramid, they'd planned how to build the first ever pyramid. 'We have got all of the supplies from the supplies hut, now let's get started.'
Days and week passed. Months and years passed and they had died. Their kids took over.
25 years later, they had finally finished the first ever pyramid. 'Isn't it beautiful?'

Ben Titterington (9)
The Gordon Schools Federation, Rochester

The Water Killer!

One bright, sunny day, in Dragon Land, there was a dragon called Water Killer. He loved his family because they played games like Dragon Monopoly. But one day he found a man called Bib! He was ugly-looking! His mother said, 'Be careful of the water, Bib! Killer can eat you.'
'Okay, Mum! I will kill him first!'
He went to kill the Water Killer, but the Water Killer was too strong and beat Bib.
Water Killer lived happily ever after with his family.
'Nooo!'...

Nestor Furst (9)
The Gordon Schools Federation, Rochester

Pirates Rising From The Dead

Sailing the seven seas, Jack Sparrow and his trusty parrot, Polly, were sailing to Pirate Mania, the only pirate restaurant.
'Hopefully the filthy mudbloods are not still there guarding Pirate Mania, thinking that it's theirs!' Jack Sparrow exclaimed. 'One day, when I have enough gold, I'm going to kill all of those muggles!' Jack Sparrow added on! 'Land ho!' Jack Sparrow shouted.
Once they got there, they were about to get off the ship when, *bang! Boom! Crash!* They fell to the ground in pain...
Two years later, all muggles were dead! How? Nobody knows...

Ria Sampla (10)
The Gordon Schools Federation, Rochester

The Future Universe

A galaxy ago there was a real threat to the future. One silent and splendid day there was a boy called Future Kid. After, his brother changed the future. Surprisingly, the Past Kid wanted it to be the past because he loved history. But his brother, Future Kid, put him in a dark haunted dungeon.

The next unpleasant day, the Past Kid escaped and took everything to the past. The only way was for Future Kid to go back to the past. Future Kid went back, changed everything back and lived happily ever after in the future.

Jude Johnson (9)
The Gordon Schools Federation, Rochester

Ancient Greece

Long ago, in a faraway land, stood a man called Joe. Joe was walking smoothly with his friend called Johnny, but Johnny wasn't an ordinary boy, he was the son of an ancient god. All of a sudden, *crash!* They went down a hole into an underground museum. Right in front of them was the magic tablet which made everyone come to life in the museum. At that second, a man wearing a blue and yellow hat and a white dress with a wristband tapped his shoulder. He turned around and screamed, 'Argh!'

Billy Hicks (9)
The Gordon Schools Federation, Rochester

Cleopatra's Saved

Once upon a time Cleopatra was locked up in the caves. A boy, called Alfie, was in the jungle and he heard Cleopatra screaming. Alfie had a horse with him and he went to get Cleopatra. There he was at the cave and he said, 'Hold on, Cleopatra.'
Cleopatra said to Alfie, 'OK.'
Alfie saved her and she said, 'Thank you for saving me.'
Alfie said, 'You're welcome.'

Chloe Randall (8)
The Gordon Schools Federation, Rochester

The Adventure

'Oh my,' said Alfie.
'It's just a field,' said Katie.
Hayden said, 'What are you two fussing about?'
'What are you doing?' Alfie said.
'Yeah, what are you doing?' said Kate.
'It's what I'm doing, not you.'
'Yeah Alfie, he's doing it, not you.'
'Let's build,' said Alfie.
'Yeah, OK, let's start now.'
'Yes, now let's put up the first rock.'
'OK,' said Alfie, 'let's go.'
'Oh no, the rock squashed you, Alfie. Are you there Alfie?'
Alfie said, 'Yes, I am here.'
'We are going to put the rock back so you are freed...'

Hayden Foakes (9)
The Gordon Schools Federation, Rochester

Caesar Combat

'Oi you, keep your hands up and you jump lightly!' Julius screeched angrily. 'We need to attack tomorrow, ready the bombs!'
They trained and trained like it was civil war against death. Finally the next day had come, they travelled to the depths of England. The first rapid, atomic, fired bombs then they charged, until the tainted defeat of England. Some fled, some died, and some survived. The British were left with nothing but food, people, some buildings and love. The Romans left and left England to die alone with the fear of death.

Aaron Uzomah Aguele (9)
The Gordon Schools Federation, Rochester

The Storm Arrives

'We shall sail the seven seas,' exclaimed Captain Joane, as he helped his slave unpack onto the boat.
'I think we are ready!,' shouted Wilbur. After a while of discussion, they set off along the coast getting further into the sea.
'How I love being at sea,' gasped Captain Joane, as he breathed deeply. He walked around the boat to his cabin to write the moment.
After a few hours, the sea turned rough and the sky went black.
'That's weird,' whispered Wilbur, as he called the Captain. Then a big swirl of wind appeared ahead of the boat.
'Argh!'

Isobelle Higgins (10)
The Gordon Schools Federation, Rochester

101

Untitled

This is a story about the Romans. They were really resilient, and never gave up. They did not like each other but worked together. One day, the emperor wanted a Roman gladiator to fight a venomous creature, which had sharp claws and a vicious stingray. It was really big. Maximus, the gladiator, geared up with aces up his sleeve, an electric rod, freeze rays and an enforcer back-up machine. He went to battle. First he put the electric rod on it and then performed a trick. Fortunately, it finally died. Hooray!

Rhys Spencer (9)
The Gordon Schools Federation, Rochester

The Mummy War

'We need to save our village!' shouted Yorb, the mummy. 'There are pirates coming to take our land!' he added.
The other mummies came rushing over to Yorb, they asked him how he knew. Yorb told them that he overheard the pirates talking about how they were going to take the land from the mummies.
At the edge of the sea were the pirates. The captain said, 'We will get that land and I will be your leader.'
The pirates were in Mummyville. The mummies saw the pirates and said, 'It's war time, Pirates!'
The mummies won the war!

Sanjana Arumulla (10)
The Gordon Schools Federation, Rochester

Lost In The Pyramid

'Oh my gosh, Leo, is that the new mum... No, I meant mummy?'
'No way! Let's go see!'
'I've got work, no time to spare.'
'Oh, come on, please let me see.'
Later on, they arrived at the pyramid of mummies.
'Ah, no, I can't handle making mummies anymore.'
'Why did you ask for the job then?'
'That's it, I'm going home.'
'Why?'
'Because I am.'
'Who shut the pyramid door?'
'No one.'
'What's that noise?'
'What?'
'Seriously, I'm scared. I think it is a mummy!'
'No way, it is just the fire crackling, see!'
'Argh, help...'

Olivia Nangle (10)
The Gordon Schools Federation, Rochester

Hulk Assemble

One day there was a man called Hulk, he was green and could smash anything you wanted him to. He was very strong and could lift anything. He was the strongest person in the world but was sometimes annoyed. He lifted things that were really heavy, he could hold a house or a swing or maybe a gigantic shed. He could probably hold a glass bottle on his head without dropping it on the floor. If it smashed it would break and people would have to go to hospital.

Charlie Langridge (9)
The Gordon Schools Federation, Rochester

Abri And The Mummy

'The mummy is awake!' screamed Abri. He fell on the floor and prayed. The mummy walked towards him. 'You will obey me!' demanded Abri.
The mummy walked towards him and bowed.
'We are going to rule the world!' yelled Abri. 'You will stay with me forever!'
He made the mummy bow to him. 'Come with me!' spoke Abri. He showed the mummy a room. 'Obey me forever, slave!' yelled Abri. Then someone touched Abri. It was a tall, dark figure. He had a big, sharp sword, it came closer to Abri...
'Argh!' screamed Abri. 'Help!'

Emma Rose Hill (9)
The Gordon Schools Federation, Rochester

Alf

It was a dark, stormy night when Brian and Lily were in the garage with their dad, Steve. Suddenly, a spaceship came from the roof. The alien was looking frightened but Lily was looking even more frightened. Mum said, 'I'm not having that monster in my house!'

'What monster, it is an alien!' Lily replied.

A couple of days passed and Mum made a mistake and called the police. Lily begged her to not say there was an alien in the house. 'Please,' she said with sad eyes. Alf the alien was lazy, but eventually went home after making friends.

Dara Stoyanova (10)
The Gordon Schools Federation, Rochester

The Seven Seas

As the boat set sail on the seven seas, the boat rocked. As the storm clapped the seas, it caused big waves and currents that were terrifying.

'What should we do, Captain?' bellowed one of the Vikings. As they turned left, waves splashed on the boat and pierced holes in the boat.

The next day, they landed on an island named Carland.

'We have to get out,' announced one Viking.

'Why?' said the captain.

'The natives,' said the Viking.

'They will have to follow our rules,' shouted the captain.

Zhi Hong Weng (10)
The Gordon Schools Federation, Rochester

Girls On The Beach

So I ran out the house and past the harbour to the beach. When I arrived, Kacey was waiting there, tapping her foot. We ran down to the rock pools, Kacey found a crab all green and spotty. She threw the poor thing into the sea. Kacey grabbed me by the arm and we spun until we both fell into the sea. We splashed and played and then I saw the sky. It was pink and the clouds were like candyfloss. Kacey looked at me and then looked at the sky. We lay in the sand until darkness was everywhere.

Ellie-Mai Woods (10)
The Gordon Schools Federation, Rochester

Pharaoh Jullian's Tomb

'Are you ready to be rich?' scoffed the tomb robber.
'Are you sure?' replied the servant.
'I think the tomb is... cursed.'
'Cursed?'
'Yes, cursed.'
'Those are just silly tales that the townspeople make up,' exclaimed the tomb robber.
'We might wake... Pharaoh Jullian,' whispered the servant.
'For the millionth time, be quiet!' boomed the tomb robber, holding his sack. The tomb robber and his servant crept up to the pyramid and walked inside the dark, gloomy tunnel. The servant took out a torch to light up the way. They saw the tomb, suddenly the light went out...

Andrew Ferguson (9)
The Gordon Schools Federation, Rochester

Untitled

One morning, Morgon and Snow crashed onto a mysterious island. They went onto the island and explored. It had Skittles, sweets and more. The best part was a bouncy castle made of jello, it was so bouncy. The island had everything, even a jello piano! Everything was perfect but soon they knew that it was time to go, however Snow wanted to stay longer, so they did!
Now it really was time to go.
'Bye-bye, mysterious island!' said Morgon.

Carys Ann (10)
The Gordon Schools Federation, Rochester

Stranded!

As Jack Sparrow woke up remembering nothing, Polly the parrot was perched on a nearby branch. As Jack stood up and looked around, he saw he was stranded on an abandoned island! Jack walked around, trying to find his way. Although he was alone, he was not afraid. Wandering helplessly, Jack began to give up hope until he saw a bright light! He began to step towards it. Then he stopped. He couldn't step through the bright light because who knows what would happen to him. Gathering all his courage, he stepped through with Polly, never to be seen again.

Joshua Achunine (9)
The Gordon Schools Federation, Rochester

The Mummy

'Mummy!' shouted Mummy's mum.
'I'm coming, Mum!' replied Mummy.
Mummy came downstairs and sat down in the kitchen. Mummy didn't have any friends and reckoned living in a pyramid was boring.
'What's for breakfast today?' Mummy asked.
'Scrambled eggs and bacon,' Mummy's mum said.
Mummy ate his breakfast and secretly sneaked out of his house. He tried to get out of the pyramid by hitting the walls. Mummy saw some traps in the distance, he thought that they might lead to the exit. He came through all the traps and bumped into someone.
'Hello, Fred.'
'Mummy.'
They introduced themselves.

Vincent Kwiatkowski (10)
The Gordon Schools Federation, Rochester

Dragon City

One sunny day, on a beach, two girls were bored. Just at that moment, Halley saw a bottle. In that bottle was a map. The girls followed where the map said to go, it took a month to find it. When they got there they heard the strangest cry. They went to see what it was: a baby dragon. The girls could see a shiny piece of food. They gave it to the dragon, he grew. The girls put on some music and started to dance. They called him Tempo.

Trinity Elizabeth Grant (9)
The Gordon Schools Federation, Rochester

All At Sea

Our boat rocked left to right, occasionally spraying me with the salty particles of the sea. I longed to go home to my family and rest in my warm bed with my wife as I watched the twinkling stars of the night sky.

'Arnal, what are you doing up on the deck at this time of night?' It was Ronald. Ronald was five years younger than me and yet it wasn't the first time he was out on the sea.

'Oh well, I couldn't sleep and I thought I could watch the stars.' Ronald eyed me suspiciously...

Jack Younger-Munn (10)
The Gordon Schools Federation, Rochester

The Mummy Is Alive!

Looking around in the pyramid, the mummy was alive, covered in bandages all white and old. The mummy stood up and walked curiously towards the pyramid door. Instead, the door was opening; the ancient queen was there. 'Who are you?' said the queen.

The mummy looked up and down and replied, 'I'm a mummy.'

'Well then Mummy, come with me,' said the queen.

Slowly walking into the palace, the mummy asked, 'Why am I coming with you?

'I need a servant so you are going to be it.'

Olivia Shanahan (10)
The Gordon Schools Federation, Rochester

The Viking Adventure

The wind blew as the boat rocked carelessly from side to side, slowly drifting forwards. 'Come on, the fish won't catch themselves,' Stoick insisted for the fourth time in a row, his ginger mane of hair flowing in the breeze.

'Fine, fine,' Astrid finally agreed and they set off. *Boom!* Suddenly, a ghostly figure appeared, shooting puffs of smoke here and there. Astrid threw her axe but it went straight through him. 'Oh no!' The figure charged at them.

After what seemed like hours later, they woke and, before their eyes, was the name in red: 'Maltagrath the Viking god'...

Magdalena Jedrzejczyk (10)
The Gordon Schools Federation, Rochester

The Weird Dragon

'Argh!' said Cery.

'Why did you scream, Cery?' said Rosy.

'There's a dragon in my room!' said Cery.

'Don't be silly,' said Rosy and walked away.

'No one ever listens to me, it's so unfair!' screeched Cery, frowning.

As the dragon got closer and closer, suddenly, *boom!* Out shot confetti from the dragon's bum!

'You are quite cute!' said Cery. 'I'll just get some food for me and you downstairs. Can I keep my dragon, Mum?' said Cery.

'Argh!' said Mum. 'Get it out of here now!'

'OK Mum, but can he stay?'

Daisy Rose Bibby (9)
The Gordon Schools Federation, Rochester

The Shore

'Sir, we have just reached land!' I said, looking across the dark, forbidden forest. 'We should get started.'
'But sir, there could be traps. People say that there are natives that don't like to be disturbed.'
'That doesn't bother me, I have an army and we will take over this land.'
'This doesn't feel right, sir.'
'Why doesn't it? We shall leave in the morning.'
I frowned and went back to my station. Just as the sun went down and darkness covered the forest, I saw something moving in the trees. I ran and found the alarms!

Ellis Dunbar (10)
The Gordon Schools Federation, Rochester

The Day At The Sandy Beach!

'Come on, come on!' Lucy shouted. But then, all of the sudden, Lucy was lost in the middle of the beach, all alone.
'Lucy, Lucy, where are you?' screamed Mum.
'I think she was overexcited,' said Dad.
'I think you're right, let's carry on looking!' sighed Mum.
'Help! Help! I'm lost!' cried Lucy. 'I want my mummy and daddy! Wait a minute, is that a mermaid?'
Out of the corner of her eye, she realised that it was a mermaid. She walked over to make friends with the mermaid. But will Lucy still be friends with her?

Katalina Espineira (8)
The Gordon Schools Federation, Rochester

Cheer Competition

'OK, get a quick drink then we'll do the pyramid,' shouted
Catherine.
After the girls got a drink, they all ran into their pyramid spaces.
'OK, and go!' Catherine said.
'Yay, you got it right, so now you can all go home for competition
places tomorrow.'
'Mum!' shouted Tia.
'Yes?' shouted Mum.
'I'm worried for competition spaces tomorrow,' Tia said.
'Well don't worry, it'll be all right,' said Mum.
'OK girls, here is the big moment, we will find out where we
came!'
'KCA Titanium, first!' said the judge.
'Yes! We won!' they shouted.

Tia Louise Conway (8)
The Gordon Schools Federation, Rochester

True Love Is Found

'More coconut water please,' Jasmine pleaded. Her servant was
called Aladdin, he had a turtle too. Aladdin had a huge crush on
Jasmine and he had always been too scared to ask her out. He
was just going to go for it and he asked her and she said yes, and
they went on the most magical date ever.
After that, Aladdin no longer worked as the servant, he was to
become a prince and asked Jasmine to marry him.

Evie Mitchell (10)
The Gordon Schools Federation, Rochester

Merlin The Magical

'Welcome, welcome, kings and queens, ladies and gentlemen, to Merlin's Magic Show!' cried Merlin, tripping over his own feet, as he spoke.

'Ha ha ha ha!' chuckled one particularly rude lord. 'This is going to the funniest show ever!'

'It is not a laughing show! It is a magic show!' screeched Merlin, his hat tipping sideways, giving him a slightly demented look.

'Enough, Rudeitar,' sighed King Arthur, 'just watch.'

'No!' screamed Merlin, the sun glinting in his unnaturally blue eyes. 'I quit! I am not a laughing stock!' he cried, fleeing from the castle, never to be seen again.

Esme Margaret Phillipson (10)
The Gordon Schools Federation, Rochester

Man Overboard!

In the sea, Captain Harrison, First Mate James and their crew were at war with General Jordan. The captain was winning, until suddenly... 'Man overboard!' the crew shouted. It was no doubt, mermaids had joined the war. The British general said, 'Men, halt!'

The pirates knew what the captain meant, but then, *splash! Bang!* 'Argh!' *Splash!* Five more men gone. More and more mermaids came up, it was just Harrison and James. Suddenly, more mermaids came up and pulled James overboard! Harrison couldn't save him. Then he saw a cannon, *bang!* His crew saved!

Harrison Dallas (9)
The Gordon Schools Federation, Rochester

113

Missing Gold!

A long time ago, in 1837, life began for me. I was born in the streets of London in a poor, little, ramshackle house but now I live in the palace as a maid. My name is Alice and I'm 21 years old. One day, all the gold in the castle was gone! I was accused and sent to the dungeons by the princess. I was shocked, the princess was my best friend. The princess' name was Katlyn. 'Katlyn, how could you think I did this? We've been friends forever!' I yelled, as the guards closed the heavy doors.

Sally Wells (10)
The Gordon Schools Federation, Rochester

Can We Get Back To Shore?

Two years ago there sat three pirates named Billy, Sarah and Hannah.
'I'm bored!' Sarah sighed.
'I've got an idea!' Billy answered. So they began to walk towards Salami Beach.
'Look, a boat!' Hannah shouted. The excited pirates went to explore it.
Two minutes later, the boat began to float away from Salami Beach. *Bonk!* 'Argh! What was that?' they all gurgled.
'We are... under the sea,' Billy screamed.
'No, no look, Hannah has just drowned!' Sarah cried. Then they all drowned. The pirates were never seen again!

Caydee-Lee Roberts (9)
The Gordon Schools Federation, Rochester

The Lost Mummy Of Egypt

'Where is he?' asked the tumber, scrambling around in cupboards.
'You lost our deceased king? Disgrace!' I said, miserably tapping my foot among the sand. 'If you don't find him, you will be buried in the desert...' I glared.
'I swear I left him right here hear the beetles,' the tumber screamed.
'OK, OK, don't yell, go find him or get a punishment.'
'I found the coffin!'
'Is the mummy in there or not?' I said.
'OK, he's not alive anymore is he?'
The coffin creaked open, it was empty, except he was now a zombie...

Jorja Tuite (10)
The Gordon Schools Federation, Rochester

The Wild Adventure!

Once there was a group of people on an adventure. Their car suddenly broke down but they had a person who was the best, called Turan. He made a house out of wood. He even made a tree house. Jordan jumped down the waterfall. He was still alive so they ate some food and they went in the sea. Suddenly, a helicopter came and got them but they decided to stayed there as they were having so much fun.
Later on, they camped in a different country but they were on a dangerous site so they returned home.

Jordan Kweku Mensah (8)
The Gordon Schools Federation, Rochester

The New Species

One day, long ago, there was a wood that had a mythical beast lurking inside! A girl called Sophie wanted to see the beast. Soon she set off on an adventure.

Soon she was in a cave of crystals, inside a wood. Inside she saw a baby dragon egg that was hatching!

A while later she saw a three-headed dragon. It was amazing, she just had to take it home. Sophie was soon home with the three-headed dragon. It was amazing!

Sophie Crosbie (9)
The Gordon Schools Federation, Rochester

The Journey To The Future!

'What are you doing?' asked Mum. Favio was getting ready to go to a rooftop party.

He asked Mum... 'All right, you can go but only if you behave.' 'Yeah, no problem.'

At the party, Kevin, Bryan, Harrison and Jordan were there but they snuck out the park where they found a time machine. They stepped inside and when they got out, they found they were in the future. All five of them got out and were fighting bad guys. They fought and fought until they finished them off with their spinning vortex move and then they went back.

Favio Sequeira (8)
The Gordon Schools Federation, Rochester

Chocolate Adventure

I set off on a magical adventure on my boat until I crashed. I found myself on a chocolate land. I thought to myself, *Should I eat it?*
I walked on and found a little house. I went over and opened the door. A cat came and scratched me on the leg. I ran home and said to my mum, 'I got scratched.'
She said, 'Are you okay?'
'Yes, I am.'

James Reach (9)
The Gordon Schools Federation, Rochester

Princess Kitty And Servant Rat

'Would you like a drink, Madam?' asked Servant Rat.
'Yes, make it quick,' replied Princess Kitty.
Servant Rat returned with a glass of coconut milk.
'You were quick,' Princess Kitty said, she was astonished.
At the moment, Princess Kitty felt a slight shake on the cruise; she had so many thoughts: should she jump or stay, or drown or survive? Servant Rat felt seasick and cannonballed into the sea.
'Um, can I have the paycheck?' screamed Princess Kitty.

Harry Dunk (9)
The Gordon Schools Federation, Rochester

Seaside Adventure!

Long ago there was a beautiful, lonely mermaid that lived with her seahorse. The two lived in an awful shipwreck in the depths of the ocean. They were very positive that they would get out of the situation.

One sunny afternoon, the two decided to take their imagination out of the ocean. Along the way they met two friendly mermaids. The three had a little talk. They said they'd found a nearby chest. 'Let's go find it!' suggested one of the mermaids.

'Yes!' answered the other.

After hours they found their gold and shared it wisely. After, they lived happily!

Mia Sanghera (9)
The Gordon Schools Federation, Rochester

Banana Bob

It was a happy day. The Minions had found the Banana Kingdom. You could hear King Bob, Emily and Dara shout, 'Banana!' They planned on having a banana pool party. Inside it was amazing, a truly remarkable sight. Bananas were everywhere. The pool was shaped like a banana, the water yellow like a banana.

Today was the pool party. The Minions wore their banana pool party suits and ate bananas while they played in the pool. Bob was happy. Emily and Dara and all the Minions were happy. This place was known as Banana Paradise, it was an amazing day.

Emily Hawes (10)
The Gordon Schools Federation, Rochester

Into The Game

One day the four gamers were creating new games when they found themselves in a game - Subway Surfers.

'Megan! Grace! Ollie!'

'Yes!'

'Evie, Who is playing us?'

'I don't know,' said Evie.

'Oh no!' said Megan.

'The boy, we can see him, look!' said Ollie.

'He's pausing the game, we have frozen. Oh, he's coming back,' said Evie and Grace.

'One, two, three... let's go!' *Bash!* They all hit a lamp post. They imagined going home and they went home in their lab and created their biggest, coolest game ever.

Grace-Olivia Putt (8)

The Gordon Schools Federation, Rochester

Rainbow Dragon!

One morning, in the Amazon, lived a polite dragon called Rainbow Dragon. One day he woke up and found out that his wings were gone.
'Who did this?' he said.
'What if Devil Dragon has taken them?' said Rainbow Dragon. The next morning, Rainbow Dragon went to Devil's house. Devil opened the door with Rainbow Dragon's wings on. A little girl then came, called Emily, and she chopped off Devil's wings. Magically, Rainbow Dragon got his wings back.
Afterwards they had a big party.

Megan Pinnick (9)
The Gordon Schools Federation, Rochester

Untitled

'This is a massive moment for me, I've been voted for school council, this is amazing.'
'Tom, hold on for a minute, there's even more good news, you got top marks in your test.'
I was so happy until I heard a massive noise. I was shocked...
'Asleep again, Tom?'
'No, I wasn't, I have special see-through eyelids.'
'OK, but at least keep them open.'
Great, Mr Fullerman had woken me up from the best daydream ever!

Adam Deans (9)
The Gordon Schools Federation, Rochester

On A Trip To Egypt!

'How are you feeling?' calmly said Lola.
'Good, how are you, Lola?' said Katie.
'I'm fine. How about we go on a walk?'
'Yeah, but where will we go?' replied Lola.
'Do you know where we are going?'
'No.'
'Have a guess.'
'Are we going to see the Romans?'
'No,' said Katie.
'Can you tell me?'
'No! You have to wait and see. It's somewhere far away.'
'Is it Egypt?'
'No!'
'Are you sure Katie?'
'Well, to be sure we are going there.'
'Yes.'
'Are we nearly there?'
'Nearly, Lola. Five minutes. We are here now, let's play!'

Katie Smith (9)
The Gordon Schools Federation, Rochester

Years of YoungWriters

YOUNG WRITERS
INFORMATION

We hope you have enjoyed reading this book – and that you will continue to in the coming years.

If you're a young writer who enjoys reading and creative writing, or the parent of an enthusiastic poet or story writer, do visit our website www.youngwriters.co.uk. Here you will find free competitions, workshops and games, as well as recommended reads, a poetry glossary and our blog.

If you would like to order further copies of this book, or any of our other titles give us a call or visit **www.youngwriters.co.uk**.

Young Writers
Remus House
Coltsfoot Drive
Peterborough
PE2 9BF

(01733) 890066
info@youngwriters.co.uk